To Mother

From

- -

$5.95

BOVRIL

ENRICHES MOTHERHOOD

For Mother
–With Love

HER SPECIAL BOOK

★★

Compiled by

PETER HAINING

PICTORIAL PRESENTATIONS
SOUVENIR PRESS

First published 1986 by Souvenir Press Ltd,
43 Great Russell Street, London WC1B 3PA
and simultaneously in Canada

ISBN 0 285 62739 2

Photoset and printed in Great Britain by
Photobooks (Bristol) Ltd.

For
my Mother
and
the Mother of my Children

'The relationship between the mother and her sons and daughters is as primitive as anything in human nature. It is on the mother's side strong, self-sacrificing, fierce if need be. It begins, at least on the side of the children, in completely dependent trust. And it continues, with many mutations, through life. Who dares to criticise a son to his mother, or a mother to her boy? The closest friendship will scarcely bear such a strain!'

The Times
10 March, 1935

'My experience shows me that Mothering Sunday is still a valued institution . . . I was actually born on Mothering Sunday, a circumstance that naturally prevented my mother from attending the annual dinner that had always been held on that day in her parents' home. And my advent, I have been told, broke up that Mothering Sunday festival!'

Cuthbert Bede
Clergyman and author, 1888

Contents

★★★

Introduction

★★

'The greatest moral force in history is motherhood. Childhood is directed by its love; youth is kept pure and honourable by its sweet dominance; and mature age finds its influence regnant, shaping character even to the end. Mother is the title of woman's supreme dignity.'

So wrote one of those anonymous scribes who compose the leader columns in that great British institution, *The Times*. Although it was written as long ago as February 1929, the words are as relevant today as they were then. Indeed, they have *always* been relevant, for as the same writer also observed, 'As "the mother of all living", Eve commands our homage.'

The place of the mother may have varied over the centuries and in different cultures, but her influence and importance have never been doubted. Without her, mankind quite simply would not be. Her vital role in history, literature and, most importantly, in our lives, is well acknowledged.

Reverence for motherhood has been evident in the history of mankind since the very earliest times, and is expressed through both religious beliefs and the equally strong power of human affection. We know, from the primitive images of mother goddesses found on ancient sites, that the religion of the Great Mother existed in prehistoric times. She represented birth, fertility, sexual union and the entire complex of life in the animal and plant world, as well as that of the human. Indeed, worship of the 'Earth Mother', as she was known in many societies, was considered paramount to survival.

In all the early civilisations there is plentiful evidence of mother-worship. The Egyptians, for example, honoured Isis, the goddess of fecundity; her Roman counterpart was Ceres, while the Greeks named her Demeter. The Great Mother, in fact, influenced all the major religions, including that of Christianity.

11

Eve—*a humorous comment on the very first mother.*

12

Mary—one of the great symbols of motherhood.

Although the New Testament did not place much importance on the position of the mother of Jesus, the cult of the Mother of God was too deeply entrenched in people's lives to permit Mary to remain in comparative obscurity for long. Today, of course, she is regarded as one of the supreme symbols of unselfish motherhood.

History is full of famous mothers whose devotion to their families or their nations have made them sources of inspiration to subsequent generations. On a humbler level, few families cannot boast of some mother whose love and sacrifice has been crucial to their well-being.

The cultures of the world have also drawn on this potent image. The second and favourite wife of Mahomet was known as the 'Mother of Believers', while the great library of Alexandria earned it the name 'Mother of Books', and the ancient city of Balkh was called the 'Mother of Cities'. Do we not speak of our native country as the 'motherland', and use the expression 'mother-wit' to describe a ready reply — 'that wit which our mother gave us', as one popular phrase would have it? And who has not heard of such fabled characters as Mother Goose, Mother Hubbard and Mother Bunch? Not to mention Mother Shipton and her prophecies, Mother Carey and her chickens and the infamous procuress Mother Douglas, about whom the less said the better!

In literature and the arts, the mother figure has had a central place for centuries, while in song and verse she has been lauded for untold generations. From the lyrical words of poets to the tunes of the concert platform or the stage of the music hall, there are examples without number of 'mother love': 'A Boy's Best Friend is his Mother', 'That Old-Fashioned Mother of Mine', Al Jolson's 'Mammy' and Izzy Bonn's immortal 'My Yiddisher Moma'.

Small wonder, then, that we should have come to honour mother with her own special day each year, in a custom that has evolved from a complex history, part-ecclesiastical and part-humane; a day called Mothering Sunday by some, and Mother's Day by others. The history, background and, indeed, confusion that surround these terms will be discussed in the pages of this book.

That this day is a much-loved tradition is indisputable. The very nature of its success is underlined by the huge number of

Mothers have been immortalised in many songs – here are four typical examples.

14

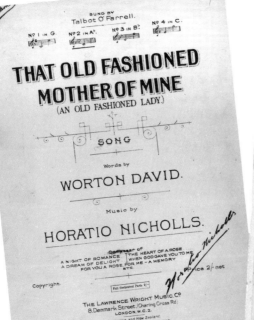

SUNG BY
Talbot O'Farrell.

Nº 1 IN G. Nº 2 IN A♭. Nº 3 IN B♭. Nº 4 IN C.

THAT OLD FASHIONED MOTHER OF MINE
(AN OLD FASHIONED LADY.)

SONG

Words by

WORTON DAVID.

Music by

HORATIO NICHOLLS.

Composer of
A NIGHT OF ROMANCE   THE HEART OF A ROSE
A DREAM OF DELIGHT   WHEN GOD GAVE YOU TO ME
FOR YOU A ROSE   FOR ME – A MEMORY
ETC.

Copyright.   Price 2/- net

THE LAWRENCE WRIGHT MUSIC Cº
8, Denmark Street, (Charing Cross Rd)
LONDON W.C.2.

Australia and New Zealand
E.W. COLE Book Arcade MELBOURNE

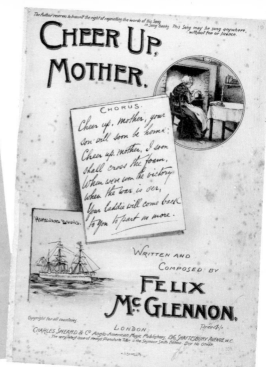

The Author reserves to himself the right of reprinting the words of this Song in Song books. This Song may be sung anywhere, without fee or licence.

CHEER UP, MOTHER.

CHORUS.
Cheer up, mother, your
son will soon be home;
Cheer up, mother, I soon
shall cross the foam,
When we've won the victory
when the war is o'er,
Your laddie will come back
to you to part no more.

WRITTEN AND
COMPOSED BY

FELIX McGLENNON.

LONDON
CHARLES SHEARD & Cº Anglo-American Music Publishers, 196, SHAFTESBURY AVENUE, W.C.
The very latest issue of Henry's Pianoforte Tutor is the Seymour Smith Edition. Buy No Other

Copyright for all countries.   Price 4/-

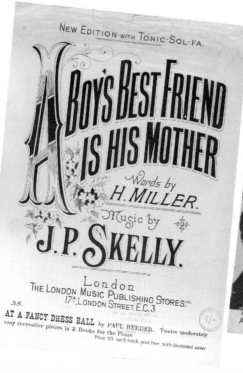

NEW EDITION WITH TONIC-SOL-FA.

A Boy's Best Friend IS HIS MOTHER

Words by
H. MILLER.

Music by
J. P. SKELLY.

London
THE LONDON MUSIC PUBLISHING STORES. Lᵗᵈ
17, London Street. E.C.3.

35.

AT A FANCY DRESS BALL by PAUL REEDER. Twelve moderately
easy recreative pieces in 2 Books for the Piano
Price 2/- each book. post free. with illustrated cover

1/-

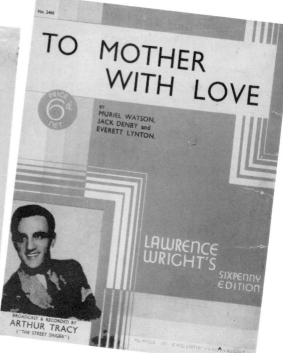

No. 2466

TO MOTHER WITH LOVE

BY
MURIEL WATSON,
JACK DENBY and
EVERETT LYNTON.

PRICE
6ᵈ
NET

LAWRENCE
WRIGHT'S
SIXPENNY
EDITION

BROADCAST & RECORDED BY
ARTHUR TRACY
("THE STREET SINGER")

PRINTED IN ENGLAND — COPYRIGHT

To Mother on
    Mothering Sunday

*And as to her we give these flowers
In token of our love,
We ask Thee, God, to add to ours
Thy blessing from above.*

A Mother's Love
An Inspirational Verse
for Mother's Day
*by Helen
Steiner
Rice*

A Mother's love
is something
that no one
can explain
it is made
of deep devotion
and of sacrifice
and pain ...

Two of the most popular cards for mothers: (left) The bouquet of violets card beloved of British children, and (right) one of the beautiful verses by Helen Steiner Rice, whose cards are best-sellers in America.

cards, bunches of flowers, boxes of chocolates and other small presents that are sold each year. As far as cards alone are concerned, the total annual sale in the United Kingdom amounts to 24.5 million, with a retail value of £10.2 million! Incidentally, the average price paid for one of these cards is 42 pence, as against 30 pence for birthday cards and 7.6 pence for a Christmas card!

But leaving such material things aside, it remains above all a day on which to say a heart-felt 'thank-you' to the woman who is probably the most influential and most loving person in anyone's life. If this little book can help you do that through its pages of information, instruction, nostalgia and not a little amusement, all brought together especially with mum in mind, then my work will have been more than worthwhile.

So, happy day, Mother — and many more of them!

Peter Haining

The Mothers of England

The mothers of this nation are generally more handsome than in other places, sufficiently endowed with natural beauties and without the addition of adultrate sophistications. In an absolute woman, say the Italians, are required the parts of a Dutch woman from the girdle downwards; of a Frenchwoman from the girdle to the shoulders; over which must be placed an English face. As their beauties, so also their prerogatives are greater than any nation; neither so servilely submissive as the French, nor so jealously guarded as the Italians; but keeping so true a decorum, that as England is termed the Purgatory of Servants and the Hell of Horses, so it is acknowledged the *Paradise of Mothers*.

And it is a common by-word amongst the Italians, that if there were a bridge built across the narrow seas, all the women in Europe would run into England. For here they have the upper hand in the streets, the upper place at the table, the third of their husband's estates, and their equal share of all lands; privileges with which other married women are not acquainted. They are also considered foremost in the raising of their children; and the esteem in which they are held by their offspring when these children grow to maturity is the envy of all other nations.

Peter Heylin (1599-1662)
Oxford divine and historian.
Cosmographie, 1652

ENGLAND
EXPECTS THAT EVERY
MAN WILL DO
HIS DUTY.

What is a Mother?

By six famous mums

****

'A mother's arms are more comforting than anyone else's.'

HRH The Princess of Wales

'My mother worked very hard all her life, and I find it sad to think that she rarely had time to relax. Children don't really appreciate just how hard their mums work until they become older and some of them become mothers, too.'

Margaret Thatcher

'A mother is the person a girl needs all her life. A boy, on the other hand, needs a father only some of his life.'

Joan Collins

'My mother taught me from a very early age to take pride in myself. You must care about yourself all the time. Self respect is the most important thing to strive for.'

Sophia Loren

'My mother passed on to me the importance of kissing and cuddling children — which I think is the thing that really matters in the end.'

Esther Rantzen

'A mother is someone to confide in, laugh with, cry with and go to when you need advice. She's someone who knows you better than anyone else does — or probably ever will.'

Nancy Reagan

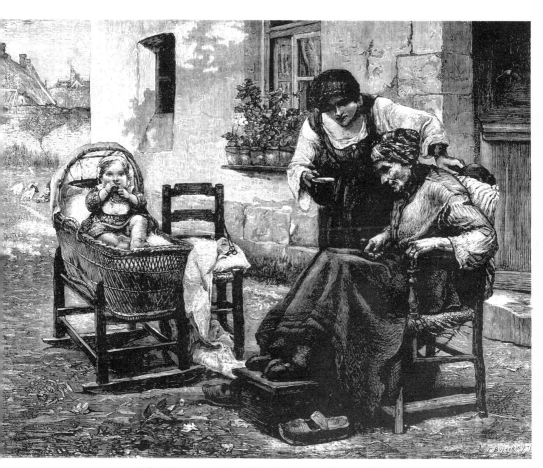

'*The Three Ages*' *from* The Sunday at Home *(1887)*.

19

Mother o' Mine

If I were hanged on the highest hill,
Mother o' mine, O mother of mine!
I know whose love would follow me still,
Mother o' mine, O mother of mine!

If I were drowned in the deepest sea,
Mother o' mine, O mother of mine!
I know whose tears would come down to me,
Mother o' mine, O mother of mine!

If I were damned of body and soul,
I know whose prayers would make me whole,
Mother o' mine, O mother o' mine!

Rudyard Kipling (1865–1936)

WHEN YOU'RE A LONG, LONG WAY FROM HOME (2).

When you're a long, long way from home, it makes you feel like you're
alone,
It's hard to find a pal that's true, that you can tell your troubles to,
And when you send a letter home, your mother's voice rings in your ears,
And then you cross the t's with kisses, what a strange world this is!
Then you dot the i's with tears, and all the sunshine turns to gloom
When you're a long, long way from home.

Mother Knows Best

★★

Every mother has her own store of home-spun knowledge that she can put to use in an emergency. Many of these tips have probably been passed on by her own mother, and not a few have the hall-mark of years of tried and tested use behind them. While any serious ailment should obviously be treated by a doctor, here are just some of the ideas that have gone to prove that 'Mother knows best . . .'

To stop bleeding, sprinkle flour over the cut. If out in the country, a cobweb applied to the blood will also halt the flow.
For bruises, sprains and inflammations, apply diluted vinegar to the injury. Ordinary treacle spread on brown paper and applied to the injury can be equally effective.
To cure hiccoughs, fill a teaspoon with brown sugar and add several drops of vinegar to it — swallow gently. Alternatively, moisten a lump of sugar and suck carefully.
Nettle sting. Rub the affected parts with a dock leaf or piece of parsley.
Nose bleeds. Hold the nose with the thumb and forefinger for ten minutes, breathing only through the mouth. Alternatively, hold an ice cube against the side of the nostril which is bleeding.
A sore throat can often be much relieved by breathing in the vapour created by a bowl of hot vinegar.
Sunburn. Although there are a great many lotions on the market, one of the most successful means of easing this condition is still a gentle bathing of the skin with sage tea.
Insect stings are best treated with ammonia or bicarbonate of soda, although honey spread over a bee sting is very effective. (After the sting has been removed, of course!)
Warts have attracted a whole range of alleged cures. Country mums reckon a daily rubbing with a fresh radish or with the juice

On Mothering Sunday

of marigold flowers can be very effective.

Headaches. There are various tablets on the market to cure these pains, but some people still maintain that betany tea, brewed from the plant gathered when it is about to flower, is the best cure of all!

Asthma sufferers have for years benefited from apple water — a mixture created by pouring boiling water over slices of apple.

Rheumatism can be effectively eased by the common dandelion. A mixture of four ounces of the plant's roots boiled in two pints of water until the liquid is reduced to one pint, and then taken by the wineglass twice a day, is the method of achieving relief.

Colds. Among the many cures offered is to sniff a little hot water up the nostrils every two or three hours.

For ear-ache, a favourite country remedy suggests wetting a piece of cotton wool in corn oil, adding a pinch of black pepper, and inserting this carefully in the ear.

Indigestion. Regular sufferers have been advised for generations to drink the juice of half a large lemon every day after meals.

Sleeplessness. The problem can be solved more easily than by counting sheep: eat a raw onion before going to bed. The soporific powers of stewed Spanish onions are said to be particularly effective.

To improve the complexion, the cucumber is said to be most effective when cut in slices, soaked in rum, and laid on the skin.

Keeping warm and avoiding getting cold are said to be the keys to good health. The back and chest should always be kept well covered when the weather is bad, while feet should be prevented from getting cold or wet.

When all is said and done, the best advice any mum can give is summed up in these words which I have heard repeated many times:

> *The surest way to health, say what they will,*
> *Is never to suppose we shall be ill.*
> *Most of those evils we poor mortals know*
> *From doctors and imagination flow!*

(Compiled from the pages of *The Lady's Newspaper* which ran a weekly column of tips from readers, from its inception in the middle of the last century until the Second World War.)

A Mother's Wish

★★

What shall I bring to thee, mother mine?
What shall I bring to thee?
Shall I bring the jewels that burn and shine
In the depths of the darkling sea?

Shall I bring the garland a hero wears,
By a wondering world entwined;
Whose leaves can cover a thousand cares,
And smile o'er a clouded mind?

What are jewels, my son, to me?
Thou art the gem I prize;
And the richest spot in that fearful sea
Will be where thy vessel flies!

Bring me that innocent brow, my child,
Bring that eloquent eye —
Bring me the tenderness, true and mild
That breathes in thy last good bye.

Mrs Elizabeth Gaskell (1810–1865)

25

A delightful engraving from the popular Victorian magazine, The Quiver.

In Honour of Mother

A history of Mothering Sunday and Mother's Day

✦✦✦

It may be interesting to put on record that one of the customs of 'Merrie England' — mothering — still survives. The fourth Sunday in Lent is the anniversary of this festival which has come from an ecclesiastical ordinance to be a family gathering. Instead of looking forward to meet in 'mother church', young people away from home look forward to this day to assemble once again beneath the old roof-tree. Servants who ask their mistress' permission to leave their duties for a few hours consider 'it is Mothering Sunday' as quite a final argument. The only accessory in connection with this institution known to me is the cake, a suspicious-looking creation, coated with white and embellished with pink. To the sorrow of many, Mothering Sunday, March 11, this year was a very wet day.

Edward Dakin
St. James' Gazette
31 March, 1888

Although Mothering Sunday and Mother's Day are often thought to be one and the same thing, they in fact fall on quite different dates and each has its own particular history and background. It is not unusual to hear people refer to the annual custom of sending cards or small presents to mothers as 'that American idea' when, in truth, it originated long before the United States was even founded.

The days can be differentiated quite simply. Mothering Sunday, the older of the two — certainly dating from at least pre-Reformation times — developed in Britain and falls each year on the fourth Sunday of Lent. Mother's Day, on the other hand, was created in America as recently as 1914 and is celebrated on the

27

28

second Sunday in May, being 'a day set aside (in the USA) in honor of mothers', to quote *Webster's New World Dictionary*. Another major reference work, *Chambers' Twentieth Century Dictionary*, notes that the term is 'also used for Mothering Sunday', and there, we can see, is how the confusion begins.

Examining the history of Mothering Sunday throws some fascinating light on bygone English customs and traditions. According to most authorities it developed 'in former days when Roman Catholic was the established religion', and it became the custom for people to visit their 'Mother Church' on Mid-Lent Sunday and there make offerings at the high altar. And it is to this custom, says the great English jurist, John Cowell (1554–1611) in his *Interpreter* (1607), 'that the now remaining practice of Mothering, or going to visit parents upon Mid-Lent Sunday, is really owing.'

The development of the tradition is supported — if not actually originated — by the Epistle of the day, which is taken from the fourth chapter of Galatians. It is an abstruse passage, in St Paul's most recondite style, but it contains the significant phrase that 'Jerusalem which is above is free, which is the Mother of us all.' (It is worth noting, too, that St Cyprian wrote, 'He cannot love God for his father who has not the church for his mother.') Thus, as another authority has put it, 'the motherhood of Holy Church and the family life of mother and children are united in one celebration.'

One can picture the scene in ancient days. Lads and girls employed on distant farms or in the service of the nobility were allowed home on this Sunday. They would carry little gifts for their mothers, and would then all go to praise God in the family pew in the parish church. Afterwards they would eat together, enjoying pieces of Simnel cake, a significant part of the custom to which I shall refer later.

Another name for this day is *Dominica Refectionis*, or Refreshment Sunday, for it was on this day that Jesus performed the miracle of feeding the five thousand and that Joseph, many generations before that, entertained his brethren. These scrip-

(*Drawn by* CAROLINE SLADER.)

(*Drawn by* F. DADD.)

THE MOTHER TO THE BRIDE.

THE MOTHER'S SONG TO HER FIRST-BORN.

tures have been claimed by certain other authorities — most prominently one Bishop Sparrow — as being the reason Mothering Sunday developed, as well as explaining why eating plays such an important role in the festivities.

In any event, the original feeling of this day is nicely caught in an extract from Robert Chambers' fine *Book of Days* (1863): 'The harshness and general painfulness of life in old times must have been much relieved by certain simple and affectionate customs. Amongst these was the practice of going to see parents, and especially the female one, on the mid Sunday of Lent, taking for them some little present such as a cake or a trinket. A youth engaged in this amiable act of duty was said to go a-mothering, and thence the day itself came to be called Mothering Sunday.

30

(*Drawn by* M. E. EDWARDS.)

CHILDREN'S VOICES.

*The three stages of motherhood
—a series of engravings also from*
The Quiver *magazine.*

'One can readily imagine,' Chambers continues, 'how, after a stripling or maiden had gone to service, or launched in independent housekeeping, the old bonds of filial love would be brightened by this pleasant annual visit, signalised, as custom demanded it should be, by the excitement attending some novel and perhaps surprising gift.'

No doubt these young people would have been surprised to learn that there is another, somewhat sinister explanation for the gifts they carried. Let me quote from William Hone's excellent *Every-Day Book* (1825):

MID LENT SUNDAY. This is the fourth Sunday in Lent, and noted as a holiday in the Church of England calendar. On this day boys went about, in ancient times,

The figure of death that partly inspired the idea of making gifts on Mothering Sunday. A picture from William Hone's Every-Day Book *(1825).*

into the villages with a figure of death made of straw; from whence they were generally driven by the country people, who disliked it as an ominous appearance, while some gave them money to get the mawkin carried off.

Its precise meaning under that form is doubtful, though it seems likely to have purported the death of Winter, and to have been only a part of another ceremony conducted by a larger body of boys, from whom the death-carriers were a detachment, and who consisted of a large assemblage carrying two figures to represent Spring and Winter, whereof one was called 'Sommerstout',

Apparelde all in greene, and drest,
  in youthful fine arraye;
The other Winter, cladde in mosse,
  with heare all hoare and graye.

These two figures they bore about, and fought; in the fight Summer, or Spring, got the victory over Winter, and thus was allegorised the departure or burial of the death of the year, and its commencement or revival as Spring.

That custom was only a variation of the present, wherein also the boys carry gifts or cakes.

Hone further suggests that the making of offerings at the altar on Mothering Sunday is derived from an ancient Roman festival, the *Hilaria*, in honour of the Mother of the Gods and made on the Ides of March.

'The offerings at the altars were in their origin voluntary, and became church property. At length the parish priests compounded with the church at a certain sum, and these voluntary donations of the people have become the dues known by the name of Easter Offerings.'

∗   ∗   ∗

Despite the evident popularity of Mothering Sunday, references to it are by no means plentiful; the earliest that has been discovered appears in a work by that poet of 'youth, love and the pagan fields', Robert Herrick (1591–1674) who, in the verses, *To Dianeme* (1648), wrote:

I'll to thee a Simnel bring,
'Gainst thou go'st a *mothering*;
So that, when she blesseth thee,
Half that blessing thou'lt give me.

Herrick was apparently describing a popular custom in Gloucester, yet it is another hundred years before anyone mentions the tradition again. This time it is the improvident poet

William Collins (1721–1759) who jokes about life in his home town of Chichester,

> Why, rot thee, Dick! see Dundry's Peak,
> Looks like a shuggard Motherin-cake.

In March 1784, however, several correspondents to the popular *Gentleman's Magazine*, 'Edited by Sylvanus Urban', were prompted to take up their pens on the subject following publication of a letter from a reader signing himself, 'D.A.B.'

> I happened to reside last year near Chepstow in Monmouthshire, and there for the first time heard of Mothering Sunday. My enquiries into the origin and meaning of it were fruitless; but the practice thereabouts was for all servants and apprentices, on Midlent Sunday, to visit their parents and make them a present of money, a trinket, or some nice eatable, and they are all anxious not to fail in this custom.

The lively response to this letter revealed that there were others who had heard of Mothering Sunday, although one writer, signing himself 'J.M.', offered a most curious explanation as to the origin of the day.

> As to Mothering Sunday of which your correspondent confesses his ignorance, this I suppose may be some Sunday near Christmas, and has reference to the Winter solstice, the night of which was called by our ancestors, *Mother-night*, as they reckoned the beginning of their year from thence.*

A Nottinghamshire correspondent fortunately put the record straight, and recalled that when he himself was an apprentice he

---

* A further unusual suggestion about the origin of Mothering Sunday — although less unlikely than J.M.'s suggestion — was offered by another *Notes & Queries* reader who signed himself 'A.H.'. 'It seems obvious,' he wrote with evident conviction, 'that Mid-Lent Sunday was so called on account of its being the day of matriculation. Not that *matricula* is of necessity a diminutive of *mater*; it more probably comes from *matrix*. Children do not go home to their mothers more on one holiday than on another.'

used to visit his mother on Mid-Lent Sunday 'for a regale of excellent frumenty.'

This 'excellent frumenty' was also mentioned by a third writer, 'O.M.', who explained on March 5 that it was a dish customarily eaten on Mothering Sunday:

> I know it is a custom in the northern counties to have Frumenty, or Furmety, as the common people call it, which is probably derived from wheat. It is made of what is called in a certain town in Yorkshire, 'kreed wheat' or whole grains, first boiled plump and soft, and then put into and boiled in milk, sweetened and spiced.

'O.M.' added that he had heard Mothering Sunday referred to in some parts of the north of England as 'Furmety Sunday', and that it was 'one of the things which probably refer to the idea of feasting or mortification according to the season and occasion.'

A fuller description of this evidently delicious dish, variously described as having a consistency mid-way between a soup and a pudding — and not far removed from a rice pudding! — is to be found in John Brady's 1815 analysis of the various traditions of the days of the year, *Clavis Calendaria*. He writes:

> A custom which was substituted by the commonality, is yet practised in many places, particularly in Cheshire, of visiting their *natural* mother, instead of the *Mother* Church, and presenting to her small tokens of their filial affection, either in money or trinkets, or more generally in some species of regale, such as frumety, fermety, or frumenty, so-called from *Frumentum* (wheat being its principal ingredient), which being boiled in the whole grain, and mixed with sugar, milk, spice and sometimes with the addition of raisins or currants, form altogether an agreeable repast.
>
> This mark of filial respect has long since been abolished in the South, though another custom to which it gave way, of the landlords of public houses presenting messes of this nature to the families who regularly dealt with them, is much within the memory of many persons yet living.

Research has shown that quite a number of other dishes were also made in different parts of Britain on Mothering Sunday. In the north and in Scotland, for instance, a dish of steeped peas fried in butter with pepper and salt was a great favourite. Pancakes made from this mixture were called Carlings, and as a result 'Carling Sunday' became another name for the day. Some authorities have suggested that the use of peas is supposed to commemorate the plucking of the ears of corn by the disciples.

Fig pies made of dried figs, sugar, treacle and spice were baked on Mid-Lent Sunday in various parts of Lancashire such as Burnley and Clitheroe, thereafter being 'taken to friends' houses in order to partake of the luxury', according to a local authority. They were also made in some parts of Northamptonshire, Staffordshire and Oxfordshire, giving rise to the term 'Fig Pie Sunday'. However, these were more properly baked on the Sunday before Easter, in allusion to Jesus' alleged desire to eat some of the fruit while on his way from Bethany on that particular day.

In some other areas of Lancashire, and throughout Cheshire, Mid-Lent Sunday was referred to as 'Bragot Sunday', after a spiced ale of this name which was drunk with slices of sweet cake. Writing about this in the *Transactions of the Historical Society of Lancashire*, the Reverend William Williams said in April 1922, 'A specially concocted drink was prepared for this Sunday which was of a non-intoxicating character and was called bragot. As the older generation passed away, the secret of its manufacture seems to have been lost, and its place was taken by mulled ale. The publicans, in later days, provided small cakes for the occasion. Every labourer expected four eggs from his employer, with which he repaired to the ale-house, where the eggs, with spices, were drunk in hot ale.'

In Gloucestershire, too, wine was distributed to servants to toast their mothers, and cakes 'coated with white and embellished with pink' were made, according to E. Walford, in *Notes & Queries* of March 1888:

One old landlady who nearly twenty years ago dispensed these 'motherings' was then over ninety, and though she has since passed away, I am told the custom still survives.

In Hereford the story was much the same, as another correspondent to the same magazine revealed. 'On the eve of Mid-Lent there were many mothering-cakes covered with white sugar to be seen in the confectioners' shop windows,' wrote J.E. Streatfield. 'The young people out at place as servants, the children at school, & etc., now go home and take their mothers one of these cakes. The good old custom was praised in the sermon at the mother church, crowded with congregation.'

Another important magazine, *The Antiquary*, reported in May 1893, that Mid-Lent Sunday was known as 'Wafering Sunday' in Hampshire after the wafer-cake marked with the impression of a seal which was given by young people to their mothers. The seal consisted of three locked hearts surmounted by a cross and enclosed within a circle. According to the magazine, the cakes were made at Leckford near Stockbridge, and a man called a 'waferer' was employed to emboss them with special iron utensils which he made red-hot over a charcoal fire.

At Bewdley, near Kidderminster, on the border between Hereford and Worcester, an interesting variation of the gift of cake was observed by Harvey Bloom, and diligently reported to *Notes & Queries*:

> The mother church of Ribsford has two porches. That on the south was known as the 'Refreshment Porch' and in it pewter plates and horn mugs were kept. On Mothering Sunday, cakes and mead were freely provided and placed ready for the use of apprentices coming home to visit friends. The food was left unguarded, but none of the townsfolk attempted to take it.
>
> The cakes were baked at Webster's in the High Street, and the mead was brewed in a large earthenware pan some two or three days previous. It was composed of oranges, lemons and spice. The whole was paid for out of the Church

Rate. It would be interesting to know if other towns made a like provision for hungry and thirsty apprentices homeward bound to their mothers.

Whether or not any other town *did* feel so moved on Mothering Sunday, there is no doubt that by far the most widely-made delicacy for this day was — and still is — the Simnel Cake.

The original Simnel Cakes—from Robert Chambers' Book of Days *(1863).*

These rich cakes, made of fine flour, are obviously of great antiquity, and the name is to be found in Early English and French as well as mediaeval Latin under the form *simanellus*. It is considered to be derived from the Latin, *simila*, fine flour, and is usually interpreted as meaning the finest quality of white bread made in the Middle Ages. However, it was evidently used by the mediaeval writers in the sense of a cake, as can be seen in such fifteenth century expressions as *Hic artocopus, a symnylle.*

In the *Dictionarius* of John de Garlande, compiled in Paris in the thirteenth century, the word *simineus* or *simnels* is used as the equivalent of the Latin *placentae*, which are described as cakes put out for sale to the scholars of universities and others. These, it is said, were usually marked with a figure of Christ or the Virgin Mary, which explains their religious significance. In later versions of the Simnel, these figures were replaced by eleven round paste balls, symbolising Jesus' faithful disciples (minus Judas), or, if they were egg-shaped, symbolising Spring and re-birth.

'Such a cake,' the historian John Nicholls wrote at the turn of this century, 'would have been a great luxury to people who rarely saw any bread other than that made of coarse meal. And by a process of culinary evolution the original simnel became the rich currant cake now known by that name.'

A description of the traditional Simnel Cake, enough to whet any appetite, can be found in Robert Chambers' *Book of Days*:

> They are raised cakes, the crust of which is made of fine flour and water, with sufficient saffron to give it a deep yellow colour, and the interior is filled with the materials of a very rich plum-cake with plenty of candied lemon peel and other good things.
>
> They are made up very stiff, tied up in a cloth, and boiled for several hours, after which they are brushed over with egg, and then baked. When ready for sale the crust is as hard as if made of wood, a circumstance which has given rise to various stories of the manner in which they have at times been treated by persons to whom they were sent as presents, and who had never seen one before — as the lady ordering her simnel to be boiled to soften it, and another taking hers for a footstool!

Perhaps not surprisingly, apart from the generally accepted facts about the evolution of the Simnel Cake, there are also a number of colourful legends concerning its birth. Two, I think, are worth retelling here.

The first gives the credit for the cake to one John Simnel, the father of the notorious imposter, Lambert Simnel, who in the fifteenth century pretended to be a son of Edward IV. After his boy's ill-fated attempt in 1487 to seize the crown with a group of 2,000 German mercenaries, John became something of a celebrity, attracting many curious customers to his shop where, needless to say, he made and sold the cakes which legend later credited to his name.

The second story is, if anything, even more fanciful.

It originated from Shropshire where, so the legend says, there lived many years ago 'an honest old couple' named Simon and Nelly, whose surname tradition does not record. It was apparently their custom each Easter to gather their children about them in the old homestead for a celebratory meal.

The couple were particular in their observance of fasting for Lent, yet always, by the end of the forty days, Nelly had managed to save a little of the unleavened dough which, from time to time, she had converted into bread. As a careful housewife, she did not like wasting a scrap and at the end of one Lenten period she told Simon she was going to use the remains as the basis of a cake to regale the family when they were all together again. Her husband eagerly seconded this idea, and reminded her that there was still some of the Christmas plum pudding in the larder.

Why not use this as the filling for the dough, he suggested, so that when the children bit through the crust they would be in for a pleasant surprise? Nelly accepted the idea readily.

However, when the good woman began to make her cake, an argument developed between the couple. He insisted it should be boiled, while she countered that it must be baked.

Soon their angry words turned to blows. Then Nelly grabbed the stool on which she was sitting and hurled it at her husband. He, in turn, snatched up a broom and began to lay about his wife.

Fortunately, before either could injure the other, Nelly had an idea — a compromise, in fact. Why should she not *boil* the cake first, and then *bake* it afterwards?

Gratefully, Simon agreed and helped Nelly set a big pot on the fire. To seal their pact, the stool and broom were smashed up to replenish the fire. Some eggs, which had also been broken during the scuffle, were used by the conscientious Nelly to coat the outside of the cake before it was baked.

Thus, says the legend, a new and tasty piece of confectionery was born, and was named after its creators. In time, only the first half of each name was employed, until these became merged from Sim-Nel to the Simnel we know today.

*   *   *

SIMNEL CAKES.

SIMNEL Cakes at Mid-Lent are analogous to Mince Pies at Christmas, Hot Cross Buns on Good Friday, or Eggs at Easter. They are commemorative Cakes, recalling the feast made by Joseph to his brethren—the account of which forms the First Lesson of the day—and also the miraculous feeding of the multitude recounted in the Gospel.

There are three kinds of Simnel Cake, named after the towns where they are said to have been first made : the Shrewsbury (or Shropshire) Simnel, the Devizes Simnel and the Bury Simnel.

The following recipe is a " Mothering " gift to England from her daughter, Canada.

CANADIAN SIMNEL.

Raisins, 1lb. ; Flour, 1lb. ; Margarine, ½-lb. ; Dark-brown Moist Sugar, 1lb. ; Egg, 1 ; Water, ¾ pint ; Cloves, 1 teaspoonful (level) ; Nutmeg, 1 teaspoonful (level) ; Baking Soda, 1 teaspoonful (heaped).

Boil the raisins in the water for 20 minutes. Rub the margarine into the flour ; add the sugar, cloves, nutmeg, soda, and the egg (lightly beaten). Then add the *boiling* raisins. Mix well, and *quickly* put the mixture into a cake tin. Bake *at once* in moderate oven for about 2 hours. When cool, cover with almond paste. Brush over with egg. Brown in cool oven.

The recipe for Simnel Cake published by the Mothering Sunday Movement in 1928.

41

Flowers have also come to play a prominent part in Mother's Day, roses and violets being the two most often associated with it.

According to tradition, in many churches Mid-Lent Sunday was known as 'Rose Day' and, to mark this, children would offer their mothers bunches of roses or else a single golden rose. This latter practice seems to have its origin in an even more ancient tradition of presenting a golden rose 'to a lady who merits it for her good deeds'. On account of the scarcity of golden roses, such gifts were usually given only to Queens or ladies of the nobility.

In church, the clergy mark this special Sunday by wearing violet or rose-coloured vestments, as the ecclesiastical historian Frederick Hall noted in his essay, 'Mothering Sunday', in 1855:

> The Church rejoiced because on this Sunday the catechumens preparing for baptism on Holy Saturday were assembled and enregistered; and the Church, as a pious mother, also rejoiced at the near approach of the time when so many new children would be spiritually born to her. Hence the whole office of the Sunday is joyful; and the altars are decorated and the ministers vested in purple.

Mr Hall also noted that in Rome, the Pope blesses a golden rose on this Sunday, the flower being a symbol of charity, joy and delight.

The universal tradition of small children giving violets to their mothers is again impossible to date, although its origins may well lie in an old English proverb which encourages the honouring of mothers in this delightful phrase, 'They that go a-mothering shall find violets in the lane.'

*   *   *

It is evident from all the examples which I have cited that Mothering Sunday has been celebrated in Britain for many centuries, but the observance was scattered, with certain areas keeping up the practice more devotedly than others. Once into the twentieth century, however, Mothering Sunday became generally recognised, and in America, where the custom persisted in certain of the communities founded by English settlers, it was put on a formalised basis — albeit on a different day — by a Congressional resolution signed by the President.

In Britain, interest in Mothering Sunday had been growing among scholars and lay-people from the closing years of the nineteenth century. This interest had taken the form of collecting details about the surviving customs associated with it, as well as a real desire among some groups to acknowledge the crucial role of the mother in family life, after all the years when she had been accorded only secondary importance to her husband. A leader column in *The Times* on 29 March, 1924 — the Saturday before Mothering Sunday — reflected this growing feeling.

We may turn now to the simpler things of home life. We are apt to think that the events which shape us are the external ones — the church, the office, the school, the shop — all that we group together as our activities. For most of us it has not been so. The real force which has shaped us was our home; that quiet background where so many happinesses were and so many calls to sacrifice. There our character was chiefly formed.

And of all the influences in the home that of the mother is the most powerful. She works, bears, smoothes, arranges, and cares for all those details which most men consider petty. It makes the whole difference to the work of life to have a well-managed and peaceful home to come back to in the evening when the day's work is done.

Yet sometimes the position and influence of the mother in the home are too little appreciated. It is all taken for granted, not least by herself. When death or sickness comes it is recognised with a pang of grief how all-important are the responsibilities she has quietly been bearing. And sometimes even the best of mothers have irritability and snubs to bear. Nothing is so sad as unavailing sorrow for things said to a mother who has gone where she cannot be told of the real but unexpected love which lay behind apparent carelessness. While we have time, let us show the tenderness we really feel.

It would be well, then, that the observance of Mothering Sunday should be revived, not only in the interests of Mother Church, but for the better understanding of the true relation between human mother and child. Family and National life would thus be sweetened.

It was a stirring and emotional call from the old 'Thunderer' — and one which was soon to be answered. A redoubtable lady named Constance Penswick Smith, of Nottingham, had been

endeavouring to interest other like-minded people in just such a national revival of Mothering Sunday; spurred on by *The Times* leader, she announced that she was proposing to form a 'Mothering Sunday Movement'. The aim of this organisation would be to 'spread a knowledge of the ancient customs of the day and their meaning'.

Mrs Smith's call for support resulted in a deluge of letters at her home in Regent Street, Nottingham, and, by 1926, her movement had not only attracted members from all over the country, but had inspired a new awareness of the old tradition. From the information she received, she was able to produce a number of publications, including *A Short History of Mothering Sunday*, *In Praise of Mother* and *Our National Mothers' Day* — 'a call to all Christian people who love their country and cherish her traditions.'

Hard on the heels of these outpourings came several specially-written hymns, including 'The Song of Thanksgiving', a rousing tune, 'Motherland', penned by one of the Movement's leading supporters, the Reverend Wesley Woolmer, and 'A Bidding and a Song' by another churchman, the Reverend W.S. Pakenham-Walsh. A leaflet describing how Mothering Sunday should be observed was also widely circulated, with these challenging words from Mrs Smith on the front: 'England, the Mother of Nations, calls to her children in every part of her great Empire to keep the Home Festival.'

To encourage children to honour their mothers, the Movement produced ribbon book-markers, pens and the very first Mothering Sunday post-cards. These had the special feature of being scented with the smell of violets! And to aid any cooks who might want to make the traditional Simnel Cake, a recipe was provided. (See facsimile on p. 41.)

Mrs Smith later wrote a Mothering Sunday play, 'full of sweet and fragrant, homely things', to be performed by children and called *The Golden Rose*. It was published in 1928, with an introduction by another supporter, the President of the Girls' Friendly Society, Lady Cecilie Cunliffe, who wrote:

In these days, when the apparent neglect of family life is threatening the foundations of our homes, Mothering Sunday needs all the support we can give it, and the love and respect due to Mothers cannot be over-emphasised. The custom of the whole family attending 'Mother' Church on this Sunday is a side of the Movement which should be encouraged, besides the gifts made for the Mother at home. All this is plainly advocated by the Mothering Sunday Movement, and this Play brings out the spirit in which these customs should be kept up.

HOMELAND.

These are the happiest hours of joy,
  No power on earth can measure,
When hearts are full, and every eye
  Is bright with beams of pleasure.

A typical early card of the type published by the Mothering Sunday Movement.

Lady Cunliffe added, 'If the observance of Mothering Sunday could be revived throughout England, a great step would have been taken towards the keeping of the Christian influence of the Home, which has been the basis of the greatness of our Country.'

The lead that the Mothering Sunday Movement had given was taken up by others — not least the confectionery trade who,

An early commercial Mothering Sunday card sold by Royle Publications.

naturally enough, saw the potential for their own business in what was happening.

At their seventh annual convention in London in April 1925, members of the Federated Association of Confectioners heard a report from the well-known confectionery maker, Sydney Pascall, that, although trade was good, new ways of expansion were urgently needed.

'The confectionery industry is of national importance and

value,' he said, 'and the term luxury trade is purely a catch phrase, mainly untrue and wholly misleading. We need to seek new opportunities for our products.'

Such an opportunity was then proposed by a Liverpool member, Mr E.L. Furber, who read a paper advocating a 'National Mother's Day' which, says a contemporary newspaper report, 'was warmly received by the audience'. A resolution that the Association should 'concentrate on the establishment of this day and that all sections of the trade be invited to work and contribute to this end' was enthusiastically adopted.

Four years later, in April 1929, at the National Conference of Labour Women in Buxton, the desire to improve the status of mothers was evidently very much in the minds of delegates, and one of them came up with the idea of forming a Mothers' Trade Union. *The Times* newspaper took an interest in the conference and carried the following report:

> Mrs Porteus, a Durham delegate, spoke on the need of children's allowances in the form of weekly payments by the State to the mothers, on a non-contributory basis. She said that she would like to see a Mothers' Trade Union, because even among their own people very often the father and sons took the mother's sacrifice as a matter of course. She was not looked upon as of any importance because she did not earn money, though she might be doing half a dozen jobs at once.
>
> While a number of delegates were in agreement with Mrs Porteus that there should be a Mothers' Trade union, they expressed wholehearted disapproval of the resolution asking that wives of trade unionists should automatically become honorary members of their husband's trade union, and the resolution was lost by an overwhelming majority.

*   *   *

While these interesting developments had been taking place in

Anna Jarvis who started Mother's Day in America.

Woodrow Wilson, the American President who established Mother's Day, photographed with his wife and their daughters.

Britain, across the Atlantic America's own special 'Mother's Day' had not only been proposed and ratified by the President, Woodrow Wilson, but was already being widely observed. As in Britain, it owed much to the hard work and efforts of one woman.

The story had begun at the end of the Civil War in 1865, and was focused around the life of Mrs Ann Reeves Jarvis, a most determined woman who was born and raised in Pruntytown, West Virginia.

Pruntytown was a typical small ranch town, except that it was sited almost exactly on the border that had divided the warring Confederate States of the North and their enemies in the South. Because of its position, some of the inhabitants had supported the Confederates and others the Northern Unionists.

After the fighting had ceased, the bitterness evident in many of her neighbours preyed on the mind of Mrs Jarvis and she determined to try and find some way of reuniting people who had formerly been friends. Her answer was to try and reach the hearts of the mothers of the soldiers. If she could encourage them to forget their enmity, she felt sure the menfolk would follow suit.

And so Mrs Jarvis started 'Mother's Friendship Day', in which she called upon all mothers who had had sons fighting on opposite sides to greet each other with the words, 'God bless you, neighbour, let us be friends again.'

The simple, direct nature of Mrs Jarvis's appeal won the hearts of the people, first in her town and then in the State of West Virginia. Within a couple more years 'Mother's Friendship Day' had spread both north and south, and had soon acquired a far wider significance.

The mothers took to wearing white carnations on this special

Two rare early American postcards which were the forerunners of the modern Mother's Day cards.

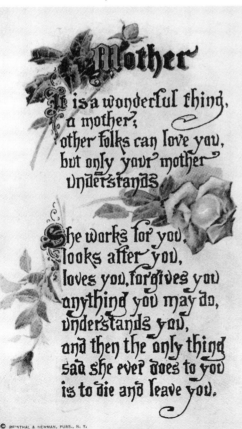

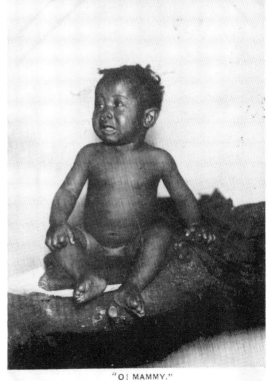

"O! MAMMY."

COPYRIGHTED, 1905, AND
PUBLISHED BY KNAFFL & BRO., KNOXVILLE, TENN.

day, to denote, 'the sweetness, purity and endurance of mothers,' as one State Governor explained it at the turn of the century.

On 9 May, 1905, Mrs Ann Reeves Jarvis died in Grafton, West Virginia, a spry old lady going to her rest sure in the knowledge of the success of her 'Mother's Friendship Day'. Her daughter, Anna Jarvis, who was then living in Philadelphia, determined to honour her mother's memory and, two years later, on 9 May, 1907, she gathered together a small group of women to mark what she called simply 'Mother's Day'.

Two typical modern cards for mum—delightful whimsy for the American market (left), and something rather more light-hearted for Britain. Both reprinted by courtesy of Valentines of Dundee.

Although the day had been intended simply to commemorate her own mother, Anna Jarvis sensed its relevance to *all* American mothers. And so, shortly afterwards, she began a campaign to have a day set aside once every year as 'Mother's Day'. The very first 'Mother's Day' was observed simultaneously in Grafton and Philadelphia on 10 May, 1908.

Six years later, the records show, Mother's Day was flourishing throughout America. All it required was Government approval to obtain official status. This Anna Jarvis determined to achieve

by taking the matter to Congress and the President himself.

On 9 May, 1914, after years of persistent campaigning, her efforts were rewarded when a Congressional resolution was signed by President Wilson in the White House, proclaiming Mother's Day, the second Sunday of every May, as an annual holiday. The dream of Anna's mother of reuniting the Civil War mothers had blossomed into a nationwide day for honouring the entire estate of motherhood.

President Wilson, whose period in office is perhaps best remembered for the amendments he made to the Constitution concerning women's suffrage, also decreed that, on Mother's Day, the American flag should be displayed on all Government buildings.

'The flag is never used in a more beautiful and sacred cause than when flying above that tender gentle Army, the Mothers of America,' he told the members of Congress.

In America, Mother's Day has since taken on several of the customs of our older 'Mothering Sunday'. Families use the occasion to spend time with their mothers, while cards, flowers and small presents are given, and the Simnel Cake (usually covered with almond paste and ornamented with scallops) has become a tradition on many a table. In truth, there is now little to differentiate the two days beyond the dates on which they fall.

But whether it is Britain, the United States or any other nation that honours its mothers, long may we all *a-mothering* go!

The Miracle of Mother Love

A Leader from *The Times*, 13 March, 1926, to commemorate
Mothering Sunday

★★

To honour one's mother is sometimes held a poor thing nowa-
days. Clever men have discovered the origin of that feeling of the
child for its mother which is falsely called its love. It is simply a
question of getting fed and cared for. The pagan cult of the Earth
Mother was simply an expression of desire for food. There is
nothing else in this boasted love and honour for the human
mother but appetite carried on, disguised but unchanged, into
maturity.

Appetite and fear, the desire for protection and the shirking of
responsibility — these are the true and the only elements in it.
And this is never to be seen more clearly than when a man comes
to take himself a wife. The thing has now become a 'complex'. He
is looking only for another woman to be a mother to him; and the
further she differs from the mother that bore him the more he will
dislike her.

So far, then, is love of the mother from being a generous and
pious emotion that it is a confession of fear and a sign of
enslavement. The clever men have analysed it all away with its
elements. They cannot be taken in; and if anyone wants to be
respected he must be very careful, if he cannot uproot any
inclination he may feel to love and to honour his mother.

Cleverness has an odd way of stopping short at a half-truth. No
lover of music will pretend that when he has analysed a perfectly
simple succession of notes by Beethoven he has proved the
passage to have no beauty, no mystery, no spiritual power. He
knows that he has no more explained the miracle than a chemist
has explained the beauty of a rose or of an opal by showing the
elements and process of their combination.

Those who attempt to analyse the human affections are for the
most part rasher than the chemist or the musician. They do not

realise that all they say may be true, and yet leave the truth unsaid. Simpler minds see more things in earth (to say nothing of heaven) than are dreamt of in their psychology.

Let it be true that in choosing a wife a man instinctively looks for someone like his mother; the plain man will only think himself lucky in being able thus to join two loves into one to the enrichment of both. Nothing would be gained by denying that the origin of love for the mother is infantile appetite; but to prove this is not to disprove the soundness, the exaltation, the vitalising power of the mature man's love for his mother. A spiritual truth can be neither disproved nor belittled by analysis.

The proper effect, indeed, of analysis should be to magnify the miracle by which the elements are exalted into the living beauty and power. And so to-morrow the plain man may, in fact or in memory, eat his fermity with a good heart, letting those call him a sentimentalist who will, because in the secret places of his soul he keeps feast on Mothering Sunday.

MOTHER'S DARLING.

Thoughts for Mother's Day

★♦★

It is a gross view of motherhood's function to regard it as nothing more than the result of contact between the sexes. There is something else than the satisfaction of passion in the mission of the woman who gives purity to the sources of life. A true marriage is something more than a regulated mode of providing the community with children. It is the expression of pure love which finds its crown in the child, who is the supreme gift to her who does not shirk the service of a larger life, and finds in it that which evokes and satisfies in an ever intenser degree the pure font of affection.

Motherhood has its marvellous power, and in it is blended pain and joy, at once the deepest and the most cleansing influence in the world. That it brings joy no one can doubt who sees the mutual love of mother and child; that there is pain in it all must recognise. Perhaps its chief grace lies in the fact that it is a ministry in which in a unique degree there is blended purposeful self-sacrifice with the confident expression of love in its purest quality. Motherhood is the paradox of life; in its fear and its resolution, its giving and receiving, at once the suppliant for our protection and the imperious monarch of our lives, it bids men pay their homage to virtue.

Christianity has always blessed motherhood, and in the Blessed Virgin Mary has achieved its glory. To whatever communion Christians belong, they do not hesitate to honour the Mother of the Lord. She clasped a child to her bosom and knew Him to be a gift from God, and every mother finds in her own divinely apportioned ministry, that which offers her the full attainment of life's purpose. We may reflect that He who was the Perfect Son must have owed much to the tender care of His mother. In infancy she fostered His consciousness of the Father in Heaven and taught Him the prayers of childhood. In later years she encouraged Him in the zeal which suffused His heart to fulfil His vocation, and although she was puzzled as time passed and felt herself smitten with a sword as her Son gave up His life on the Cross, the reward which comes to those who faithfully fulfil the appointed ministry of motherhood was given to her in her participation in what her Son accomplished for the world.

So motherhood enlarges the life it gives and, by allying itself to the recreating life of the Divine Spirit, with all that is true and good, has its part in the redemption of the race.

New York Times,
10 May, 1929

3315

Happy Families

To the Editor of *The Times*

Sir, While your correspondents concern themselves with trivial matters, such as the names and designer of those so-called 'Happy Families' cards, may I pose a fundamental question? What right have these families to be considered happy when not a single one of them has more than two children?

Doubtless that is felt to be happiness in this self-indulgent and degenerate age, but the great days of Queen Victoria knew better. It is such thoughtless lapses as this which stamp upon the Victorian era the undeserved stigma of hypocrisy.

Yours,
A Mother of Eight

The Times
13 December, 1939

IT'S ALL IN A LIFE TIME.

Pearls of Mother

One hundred of mum's favourite sayings

★★

Everyone remembers those little pearls of wisdom that their mothers imparted when they were young. Whether they were sound nuggets of advice based on a lifetime's experience (or else handed down from their own mothers or grandmothers) or merely the kind of mad-cap logic that parents sometimes feel compelled to use on children, these little sayings have a durability all their own. The list below may provide some nostalgic amusement for mothers — or their sons and daughters — by reminding them of the advice that was formerly handed out to them, or by introducing them to sayings that others had to listen to.

I am grateful to the following people for searching their memories to provide these lines: my own mother, of course, and my wife; Henry Cooper, Su Pollard, Tommy Docherty, Linda Lusardi, Rula Lenska, Shirley Williams, Vivien Neves, Bryan Robson, Jimmy Savile, Eric Bristow, Graham Gooch, Danny La Rue, Ernie Wise, Sophia Loren, Wayne Sleep, Roy Hattersley, Paul Daniels, Cyril Smith, Ray Reardon, Faith Brown, Keith Waterhouse, Eddie Large, John and Margaret Kent, Frank and Linda Peacock, George and Judy Butcher, Brian and Jan Strudwick, Gillian and Mike Hill, George and Sue Farrow, Eve and Lou Wilkes, Pamela Chamberlaine, Bill Lofts, Frank Parnell, Geoff Waring, Gerry Battye, Tessa Harrow and Ernest Hecht.

1   The most wonderful thing in the world is to have someone to whom you come *first*.
2   If at first you don't succeed, try, try again.
3   Just *wait* until your father gets home!
4   Save a little, spend a little. And remember — You get owt for nowt.
5   It doesn't cost anything to use a bit of soap. Cleanliness is next to Godliness.

No cartoonist has better caught the nuances of mother-and-child relationships than Field Smith, whose jokes delighted readers of Pearson's Magazine *for almost half a century. The examples on these pages are from 1922, 1924, 1927 and 1930.*

MOTHER: "Gentlemen never hold their knives like that, Bobby."
BOBBY: "And ladies never watch people eating, Mummy!"

6   I'm not asking you — I'm *telling* you!
7   They can take away your job, but they can't take away your ability.
8   You will only be respected if you respect yourself.
9   You're not the only pebble on the beach.
10   If your mum doesn't care most about you, *who* will?
11   You treat this house like a hotel!
12   A mother learns as much from her children as they learn from her.
13   Never let the sun go down on your anger.
14   You can't start the day on an empty stomach.
15   Nothing lasts forever. Just because the world's at your doorstep — don't drift off onto cloud nine.
16   What I say is, you can choose your friends, but you can't choose your relatives.

17 If you keep making that face and the wind changes, it'll *stay* like that.
18 If you eat too many lollipops you'll turn into one.
19 Who's the 'she' you keep talking about? The cat's mother?
20 So it's raining? You won't melt!
21 Don't ask me why — the answer is NO!
22 That spot will never get better if you pick it.
23 I wouldn't trust (him/her) farther than I could throw them.
24 Everybody *else* may be doing it — but *you* are not going to!
25 Take that hair out of your eyes!
26 It's no use crying over spilt milk.
27 Don't worry about it, dear, there are plenty of other fish in the sea.
28 Always remember the three B's — be good, be careful and BE HOME EARLY!

"Mummy, what is 'blast'?"
"Blasting, child, is used in finding coal and slate and—ahem!—collar-studs."

29 It's not the clothes you wear — but the person who is in them.
30 Always wipe the toilet seat before you sit on it.
31 You seem to think that rules are only made to break!
32 How is it that you only help with the washing-up at *other people's* houses?
33 All your chickens will come home to roost.
34 You can't read and eat at the same time.
35 You can't judge a book by its cover.
36 You won't be happy until you're crying!
37 Never talk to strangers.
38 You've made your bed — now you can lie on it!
39 Remember — two wrongs don't make a right.
40 You only nag the ones you love.
41 Silence is golden.
42 Well, pardon me for breathing!
43 Never go out without clean underwear in case you are involved in an accident.
44 Why do *you* think I've got all these grey hairs?
45 No one ever got a job with dirty fingernails.
46 Finish up that food — there are starving children in Africa.
47 This is going to hurt *me* more than it hurts you. I'm only doing it for your own good!
48 If you can't be friends with your brother/sister, how can you expect to get along with anyone else?
49 There's no such word as 'can't'!
50 Close that door! Were you born in a barn?
51 The way to a man's heart is through his stomach.
52 If you keep crossing your eyes, they'll get stuck like that.
53 Put that down — you don't know *where* it's been!
54 Just because daddy and I can do something, that doesn't mean *you* can!
55 You can't make a silk purse out of a sow's ear.
56 You *must* make your bed — in case the house burns down!
57 Only your mother will tell you the truth!
58 If that medicine didn't have a horrid taste it wouldn't be

SMALL BOY (viewing rabbit with young): "Mummy, who teaches rabbits their multiplercation tables?"

doing you any good!
59 I knew he/she wasn't the right one for you!
60 Sit up straight at the table!
61 If someone stuck their head in the gas oven, would *you* do the same?
62 Don't do as I do, do as I *say*!
63 A lady never sits with her legs apart.
64 Don't turn your nose up at things.
65 You have to suffer to be beautiful.
66 The bigger you get the more stupid you become!
67 You don't have to like me — *I'm* your mother!
68 Why don't you go out and play on the motorway?

69 Close your mouth — there's a bus coming!
70 You're no oil painting!
71 A little of what you fancy does you good.
72 Don't worry — it's only puppy fat.
73 Eat it all up — it's good for you.
74 But the crust of the bread is the *best* part!
75 You should chew every mouthful 75 times.
76 I can't be in twelve places at once!
77 Don't go to sleep after a meal or you'll get fat.
78 The girl who marries for money has to earn it.
79 A man sweats — a lady glows.

MOTHER : " Joan, dear, don't climb about all over everything. When shall I teach you to sit like a lady ?'

80 Hurry up — quick's the word and sharp's the action!
81 Keep your chest out and your stomach in. A long walk will put colour in your cheeks!
82 A fool and his money are soon parted!
83 There are only two things in this world you can be sure of — we all need money and your mother loves you.
84 If a thing's worth doing — it's worth doing *properly*.
85 *Who* do you think is paying for all this, anyway?
86 Don't sit so close to that television — you'll ruin your eyes!
87 You have to get up early in the morning to outsmart your mother.
88 As long as you live in my house you'll do as *I* say.
89 Cheer up — your time will come.
90 Girls are like buses — there'll be another one along in a minute.
91 Is that a threat or a promise?
92 You can't have anything else until you've finished your vegetables.
93 How *can* you live in such a pigsty?
94 Wash behind your ears — or else you'll have potatoes growing there.
95 You've got a face only a mother could love!
96 If I had talked to my mother the way *you* talk to me . . .
97 You think you've got an answer to everything, don't you?
98 If you can't think of anything nice to say, don't say anything at all!
99 You kids will be the death of me!
100 In the end, *love* is all that matters.

Advice to Mothers

From *The Mother's Friend*, 1860

★★★

The Home-Mother

We must draw a broad line between the home-mother and the frivolous butterfly of fashion, who flirts from ball to opera and party, decked in rich robes, and followed by a train as heartless as herself — she who, forgetful of the task assigned her, neglects those who have been given to her charge, and leaves them to the care of hirelings while she pursues her giddy round of amusements. Not so with our home-mother! The heart warms to see her in her daily routine of pleasant duties. And how proud and pleased is each little recipient of her kindness. Her children will rise up and call her blessed, and the memory of her kindly deeds will enfold her as a garment.

Be a Friend to your Child

Where shall your child go for sympathy and counsel but to yourself? Does it run to its parent with its little cares and difficulties, or has it been taught to feel that they are too small and insignificant to enlist their mother's attention and sympathy? If the latter, you need not wonder if you meet a rival in its affections. Be its friend, enter tenderly into its minutest sorrows, anxieties, and plans, and thus reserve for yourself the dignity of counsellor, parent and friend.

The Cause of Early Mortality

A popular writer contends that one-fifth of the children born die before they attain one year old — and significantly asks, if a farmer was to lose one-fifth of his cattle, would he not ascertain the cause and apply the remedy? Children are over-fed, over-clothed, take too little exercise in the air; and these are the causes of mortality among them. We agree with the writer who recommends mothers to study Combe and Brigham instead of Bulwer

67

THE

MOTHERS' FRIEND.

EDITED BY

ANN JANE.

"JUST AS THE TWIG IS BENT, THE TREE'S INCLINED."

(VOLUME THIRTEENTH.)

VOLUME I.—NEW SERIES.

London:

WARD & CO., 27, PATERNOSTER ROW, E.C.

1860.

and Boz! (*Editor's note*: George Combe and Walter Brigham were two early pioneers of popular education, while Edward Bulwer Lytton was the author of hugely successful novels and Boz was, of course, Charles Dickens.)

Be Careful, Mother!

A few sharp, hasty words, and Mr and Mrs Smith parted until dinner-time. As this was certainly not the first time this had occurred, Mrs Smith soon forgot the circumstance, and commenced humming a tune, when the angry voices of her children attracted her attention. 'O! how naughty to quarrel,' she exclaimed, 'you should never do that.' 'But you and papa quarrel,' was the quick reply of a bright boy of six. The mother could say no more; she was reproved for the moment.

Deal Honestly with Children

Dissimulation should never be practised before children. If you would have your children grow up frank, honest, ingenuous, deal honestly with them. No practice is more reprehensible than that of threatening or making promises to children which you never fulfil. The example of the mother has much to do in forming the character of the child. Any child that is subject to continual deception, is almost sure to practise it towards others. Make honesty of purpose, speech and action natural to him or her. This you can do by correct example and affectionate precept.

The very popular Mothers' Friend *from which these extracts were taken.*

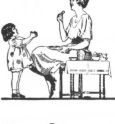
More good advice for mums—some rather striking advertisements from the Nineteen-twenties.

Mother's Book of Records

★★

According to the *Guinness Book of Records*, the British mum to have given birth to more children than any other was Elizabeth Mott of Monks Kirby, Warwickshire, who married in 1676 and by the time of her death in 1720 had produced no less than 42 offspring! The oldest mother in these islands was Mrs Winifred Wilson of Eccles, Greater Manchester, who was 55 when she gave birth to her tenth child, a daughter, in November 1936. While the mother to leave the largest number of descendants was Mrs Sarah Crawshaw whose grave in Stones Church, Ripponden, Halifax, West Yorkshire, reveals that there were no fewer than 397 of them alive when she passed away on Christmas Day, 1844.

These are just three of the straightforward records that British mothers have achieved over the years. There have, though, been a number of rather more unusual ones that have yet to find their way into the record books . . .

✣   ✣   ✣

THE ENORMOUS BABY

The world's fastest growing child was Thomas Hills Everett, the fifth child of Mrs Jane Everett and her husband George, of Enfield, Middlesex, who was born on 7 February, 1779. At the time of Thomas' birth his father, a paper mill owner, was 36, and his mother 42. According to contemporary accounts, neither was above average size, and all their previous children — the eldest of whom was then twelve — had grown normally.

The baby was of 'average' size at his birth, according to his mother, but at six weeks began to grow prodigiously. After nine months his extraordinary development came to the attention of a local doctor, Mr Sherwin, who was so amazed at Thomas' size

Thomas Everett, the bouncing baby, at eleven months old, with his mother, Jane.

THOMAS HILLS EVERETT,
Aged Eleven Months.

that he measured him against his own well-developed seven-year-old son and forwarded the details to the Royal Society in London.

These figures revealed the baby Thomas to be two foot around the chest, as against the boy's 22 inches. His thighs were 18 inches, almost five inches thicker than those of the boy, while his calf was 12 inches as against nine inches. Around the wrist, Thomas measured six-and-three-quarter inches compared with four-and-three-quarters and, around the elbow, at eight-and-a-half inches he was a full two inches thicker than the doctor's son.

Mr Sherwin reported that the mother 'entertained a vulgar prejudice against weighing children', so he had guessed the weight at nine stone. The infant's height was three feet and a quarter, and he was entirely breast fed!

Sherwin described the baby as being uncommonly good tempered and having 'very fine hair, pure skin, free from any blemish, was extremely lively and had a bright, clear eye'. His head was small in proportion to the rest of his body, but he had 'rather more expression in face than is usual at his age'.

'It was impossible,' concluded the doctor, 'to be impressed with any other idea than that of seeing a young giant.'

In fact, the Everetts decided to exhibit their 'Enormous Baby' in Holborn, London, where the print reproduced here was made in January 1780, when he was eleven months old. Sadly, and despite Mr Sherwin's belief that Thomas was 'as likely to arrive at maturity as any child he ever saw', the unfortunate baby did not long survive the rigours imposed upon him by the huge crowds who flocked to see him, and he died aged 18 months.

Footnote: The largest recorded live birth weight in Great Britain is 21 lbs for an unnamed child born on Christmas Day, 1852, in Torpoint, Cornwall. In 1935, a boy of two years and nine months was reported by the *British Medical Journal* to weigh seven stone two-and-a-half pounds.

✳   ✳   ✳

THE MOST MARRIED MOTHER

The dubious distinction of being the world's most married mother belonged to a petite blonde Sheffield woman named Mrs Theresa Vaughan. Her astonishing record came to light in December 1922, when she was brought before the Sheffield Police Court charged with bigamously marrying a local man.

During the course of her trial Mrs Vaughan — who was then only 24 years old! — confessed that she had married a total of 61 times without obtaining a divorce from her first husband. She said that her 'husbands' were scattered all over the British Isles as well as in Europe, and even as far away as South Africa. She had gone through wedding ceremonies with all these men in the space of just five years.

As a result of the hearing, the luckless first husband was granted a divorce. The sole child of this marriage — a girl — perhaps influenced by her mother's unsurpassed record, never married at all!

Footnote: The most monogamously married English woman is Olive Joyce Wilson of Marston Green, Birmingham, who has had eight husbands; while the world record is held by Mrs Beverly Nina Avery of Los Angeles, California, who divorced her fourteenth husband in October 1957 when she was 48. Two of her husbands she had actually married twice!

*   *   *

THE MOST AMAZING MOTHER — 1

Mothers have claimed some amazing births over the years, but surely none more incredible than that of Mary Tofts who in 1726 declared that she had given birth to a litter of rabbits! Although the story was subsequently shown to be a hoax, it has no equal in the history of motherhood.

Mary was the wife of a clothmaker in Godalming in Surrey, and in the year of her 'confinement' was described as being small in size, with a fair complexion and a healthy, strong constitution. She was also said to be unable to read or write and had 'a very stupid and sullen temper'.

Stupid she may have been — but for some considerable time her claim to have given birth to rabbits was widely believed.

The actual birth was said to have taken place just before Christmas, 1726. According to a contemporary report, this 'monstrous deviation from the laws of nature' had resulted from events which occurred while Mary was working in a field earlier in the spring.

'As she was weeding with some other women,' says the account, 'she saw a rabbit spring up near her, and this set her a-longing for rabbits — being then, as she thought, five weeks gone with child.

'Soon after, another rabbit sprung up near the same place, which she endeavoured to catch. The same night she dreamed that she was in a field with those two rabbits in her lap, and awaked with a sick fit which lasted till morning.

'From that time, for above three months, she had a constant and strong desire to eat rabbits, but being very poor and indigent could not procure any.'

Mary's life changed dramatically, however, after the 'birth' of the rabbits — a fact which was 'authenticated' by her medical attendant, a Mr Howard who had practised for thirty years. According to his report, he 'aided her to bring forth nearly twenty rabbits'.

Despite the incredibility of the 'birth', news of it soon spread far and wide, even reaching the ears of King George II who sent his surgeon, Mr Ahlers, down to Godalming to investigate. The good doctor returned to London, 'fully convinced that he had obtained ocular and tangible proof of the truth of the story — so much so, indeed, that he promised to procure for Mary a pension,' says another account.

The King's surgeon and anatomist, Mr St Andre, was also sent to make an examination and returned equally convinced. He even dissected a couple of the rabbits in front of King George to prove they were real.

A detailed report of 'Mary Tofts, the Rabbit Breeder' was then published and created a storm of controversy. There were as many earnest believers in the tale as there were disbelievers, and pictures and pamphlets of the affair sold in huge quantities.

Although King George persisted in his belief in Mary's story, it was his wife, Queen Caroline, who brought about the exposure of the fraudulent birth. For when the 'miraculous young mother', as she became known, was brought up from Surrey to London for further tests by the eminent physician, Sir Richard Manningham, the Queen proposed that her womb should be examined.

'At this threat of a dangerous operation upon her,' says another later report, 'her courage was shaken, and when the threat was backed by another from a magistrate that it must be performed or

*Mary Tofts of Godalmin
the Pretended Rabbit Breeder*

*Two contemporary pictures of Mary Tofts,
the 'mother of rabbits'.*

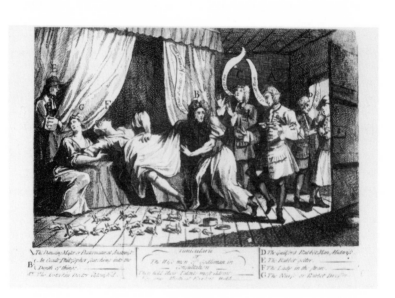

she should be sent to prison, Mary Tofts confessed.

'She said the fraud had been suggested to her by another woman who told her that she could put herself into the way of getting a good livelihood without being obliged to work. The other woman promised to supply her with the rabbits for which she was to receive part of the gain.'

And so the 'Rabbit Breeder', who had successfully convinced hundreds of thousands of people of the truth of her claim, was finally unmasked. The details of this most amazing 'mother' remain enshrined not only in the records I have cited, but also in the two contemporary engravings opposite.

*   *   *

THE MOST AMAZING MOTHER — 2

A competition to find 'The Most Amazing Mother' was held in the town of Etobicoke near Toronto in Canada, in September 1983, and produced a deserving, if unfortunate, winner. The top mum, Mary Downsview, was entered by her daughter, Tamara, who described her thus:

> I will conceal certain unpleasant details of events in my mother's life, but at the age of 13 she was laid low with arthritis. Since then she has had four strokes, lost both kidneys and suffered a brain haemorrhage.
>
> She also emerged from a sixty-day coma not knowing her own age, or that she was married with two children. On her lips was the word, 'Pray'!
>
> Shortly afterwards she developed cancer of the tongue, had her thyroids removed and supported a mysterious disease called *lupus* — which attacks every organ in the body. Recovering from these handicaps, she had a kidney transplant, after which the doctors and nurses described her continued existence as 'a miracle'.

Miss Downsview ended her citation by reporting that her

mother now had two plastic hands which nonetheless enabled her to 'cook, do her housework and hold aloft her two grandchildren, looking into their eyes with ecstatic love'.

*   *   *

THE RECORD SLEEPER

A group of noisy, boisterous children are believed to have caused their exhausted mother to fall into the longest sleep on record. This hard-pressed woman was Mrs Elizabeth Perkins, who lived in the tiny, picturesque village of Morley St Botolph near Attleborough in Norfolk. The wife of a farm labourer, she was in her late thirties and the mother of eleven children, all of whom lived in a three-roomed tied cottage on land belonging to Morley Hall.

Mrs Perkins' brood of children — seven girls and four boys ranging in age from a baby to several teenagers — had apparently been confined indoors by torrential rain during the month of July 1788 when the events in question occurred.

According to a somewhat later report, Mrs Perkins was a good, if somewhat nervous mother, and the high-spirited and occasionally argumentative play of her children had taxed her patience considerably.

Quite suddenly, on the morning of 20 July, she complained to the eldest child, a girl, of all the racket going on in the house, and said it had so tired her that she must lie down for a while. At this, she took to her bed and fell into a deep sleep.

She was still asleep when her husband returned from the fields at dusk. Anxious for his dinner, he chided his children for not waking their mother, but neither they nor he could rouse her.

By the next morning, when she had still not woken up, Mr Perkins and his family became worried and summoned the local doctor. But, as a contemporary account notes, 'not all the stratagems, nor medical arts, could rouse her; and in this silent state she remained for the long period of *eleven days and six hours.*'

78

ELIZABETH PERKINS.

Published by G. Smeeton, St Martins Church Yard, March 1st 1820.

Elizabeth Perkins, the amazing sleeping mother!

When she awoke, 'to the great joy of her numerous relatives and to the wonder of the neighbourhood where her profound sleep had become all the talk', she was quite unaware of how long she had slept. Nor could she account for it — beyond the exhaustion brought upon her by the children.

On 26 July, while she was unconscious during her marathon sleep, the portrait reproduced here was made of her and later published with an account of the events.

After awaking, Mrs Perkins returned to her normal duties as a housewife — although now in a somewhat quieter house, the children having been thoroughly alarmed by what had happened to their mother — and for some time thereafter she slept quite normally. However, it seems her health must have been affected

79

in some way, for two years later, in 1790, she died.

To this day, no completely satisfactory explanation for this harrassed mother's inordinately long sleep has been put forward . . .

Footnote: Curiously, the record for the longest period of going voluntarily *without* sleep is held by another mum, Mrs Maureen Weston, from the neighbouring town of Peterborough in Cambridgeshire, who stayed awake from April 14 to May 2, 1977 — a total of 449 hours — in order to win a Rocking Chair Marathon!

✻   ✻   ✻

EPITAPH TO A GREAT-GREAT-GREAT-GREAT-GRANDMOTHER!

In the little parish church of Maltby le Marsh, not far from Mablethorpe in the county of Lincolnshire, there stood for many years a tombstone commemorating a most remarkable grandmother.

The grave marked the last resting place of Ema Dalburg, a member of a distinguished Lincoln family, who, at the time of her death in 1851, was a great-great-great-great-grandmother. Her descendants to the sixth generation were present at the funeral, a fact recorded in local history as well as in the lines which were inscribed on her tomb. These read:

> The mother to her daughter spake:
> 'Daughter,' said she. 'Arise!
> Thy daughter to her daughter take,
> Whose daughter's daughter cries!'

Footnote: In the last twenty years, at least half a dozen great-great-great-great-grandmothers have been reported, the most recent being Mrs Ann Weirick of Pennsylvania, who was 88 years old when she heard of the birth of her great-great-great-great-grandson, appropriately named Matthew Stork, in September 1976!

THE ULTIMATE SLIMMER

On the Cleveland Hills not far from Guisborough, where the bracing North Sea winds blow in across North Yorkshire, lived the mother who could well have claimed to have devised the ultimate slimming course. For Eve Fleigen, a grotesquely over-weight seventeen-stone mother of four, became a slim nine-stone beauty on a diet of wild produce, in particular flowers!

Eve was married to a Yorkshire landowner, and by continual over-indulgence had, by the year 1805, acquired a figure that could only be described as mountainous. Not only did her

Eve Fleigen who lived on a diet of flowers!

husband and children complain about this, but also her step-mother who lived with the family and had been trying for years to curb her excessive eating.

Eve was finally brought to her senses when she found herself forever short of breath and barely able to move in comfort. She vowed then to take some drastic action.

Her solution was a diet consisting of a few berries and wild fruits, but primarily the leaves and petals of edible flowers. In the space of a year she was unrecognisable, and the fame of the 'diet' which she had used spread throughout the North of England.

So pleased was Eve with the result that she wrote the following lines to be placed on her tomb when she died, a robust seventy-year-old:

> 'Twas when I prayed I never might eat more,
> Because my stepmother grudged me food,
> That on flowers I fed, as I had store,
> Or on a dew that every morning stood,
> Like honey on my lips, full seventeen year.
> This is the truth, if you the truth will hear.

Despite the apparent success of this diet, the reader is advised *against* following the example of the 'Woman who Lived on the Smell of Flowers', as tradition has named her!

*   *   *

DEATH OF A CHILD FROM ITS MOTHER'S MILK

Surely the most curious death on record is the following one recorded by a Professor of Medicine, Christopher Hufeland (1762-1836), in his book, *Makrobiotik* (1796):

A person of Munster in Ireland quarrelled with a soldier who lodged in his house. The latter drew his sabre and attacked his host whose wife, terrified at the danger to her husband, rushed on his adversary, wrested the weapon from his hand, and threw it to a distance.

82

By this time others had arrived, and the combatants were separated. The woman then, being still greatly agitated by the occurrence, took her infant, which was quite well, out of his cradle, and applied it to her breast.

The child quitted the nipples with marks of inquietude, sighed, and became lifeless in the mother's arms. Dr Tourtual, of Munster, was called within a quarter of an hour, and administered all the assistance in his power, but without avail.

The influence of the mother's milk on the child has long been known. The passions of the nurse, in particular, are unfavourable to their infants, who are all affected under such circumstances; restlessness, colic, diarrhoea, vomiting, & etc.; but we are not aware of any case similar to this one in which the milk would seem to have acted as a quick and powerful poison.

✻   ✻   ✻

DIED FROM TIGHT CORSET!

Another strange death is recorded of an unfortunate Bristol mother who, in January 1851, died from lacing her stays too tight!

According to an inquest held by the Bristol Coroner, Mr Grindon, the woman, Mrs Alice Oliver, aged 22 and a mother of three children, had at the time been desperately trying to regain her figure after the birth of her latest child.

The Coroner had, he said, instituted a very careful *post mortem* examination, and the medical testimony clearly showed that the deceased was perfectly clear from disease.

'There was no other visible cause of death except the compression of the stomach and viscera from tight lacing,' said Mr Grindon. 'Her death was, in my opinion, caused by — or at least much accelerated by — the pernicious practice of tight lacing, in which so many of her sex foolishly indulge.'

The unhappy Alice Oliver who was squeezed to death by her corset!

The jury duly returned a verdict that the death of the unfortunate Mrs Oliver was caused by 'idiopathic asphyxia, hasted by tight lacing'.

*   *   *

'A WOMAN WITH CHILD FOR 27 YEARS'

Surely the most bizarre record to be found in the annals of motherhood concerns Ann Smith, the wife of a Suffolk tailor, who, according to *The Wonderful Magazine* of January 1793, was 'with child for 27 years'. The story goes:

The wife of a certain tailor of Bungay, having been married twenty years, without ever having a child, thought she perceived in herself some signs of her being with child. About the common time, she felt the usual pains of child-bearing, but could by no means be delivered.

She kept to her bed for three years, with the pains of labour continually upon her. At the end of which time her pains ceased, but her belly remained big until her death, which was not till twenty-four years afterwards.

When being opened after her death, a female infant was found within her, perfectly formed and petrified. This woman lived in the time of Henry III, about the year 1250.

Mother's Love

My mother's eyes! — when shall I see
Again those dear eyes turn'd on me?
My mother's voice! — when shall I hear
That more than music to mine ear?
My mother's hands! — when shall I press
Those gentle hands in sweet caress?
My mother's lips! — when shall I prove
How sweet the kiss of mother's love?
My mother's faithful bosom, too,
The only one for ever true:
When shall my fever'd head repose
Upon that kind, that tender breast;
And there in balmy stillness rest,
Oblivious of life's blighting woes?

Anonymous
Faithful Words, May 1837

Dead! and . . . Never Called Me Mother

Some memorable quotations on the state of motherhood

★★

Literature is full of memorable references to mothers — good mothers and bad, pretty mothers and ugly, much-loved mothers and those who have earned only the enmity of their family, relatives and friends. To attempt to bring all such quotations together would prove an almost impossible task, but here is a representative selection of some of the best-known and most interesting, complete with their sources — for although a number of them may be familiar to the reader, it is a fact that those who use them in everyday conversation are often quite unaware how or where they originated.

One example, arguably the most famous quotation of all, is:

Dead! and . . . never called me mother.

Although this is widely credited to have appeared in the hugely-successful novel *East Lynne*, written in 1861 by Mrs Henry Wood (1814-1887), nowhere in that book is it to be found. In fact, the line was invented by T.A. Palmer for the stage version of the story when it was put on in London in 1874.

Among the timeless proverbs which are passed from generation to generation are at least two especially worth noting:

He that would the daughter win,
Must with the mother first begin.

This was collected by the English naturalist John Ray (1627-1705) for his book *Proverbs* (1670). Ray also noted this very familiar saying:

Like mother, like daughter.

James Howell (1593-1666), who spent a decade as a Royalist

spy and after the Restoration was made Historiographer-Royal, is credited in 1659 with one of the earliest mother-in-law sayings:

The mother-in-law remembers not that she was a daughter-in-law.

Among the works of that prolific writer, Anonymous, is to be found this gem:

> *Lizzie Borden took an axe*
> *And gave her mother forty whacks;*
> *When she saw what she had done*
> *She gave her father forty-one!*

Lizzie was, in fact, a young lady charged with murdering her stepmother and father at Fall River, Massachusetts, in August 1892. She was, however, acquitted.

According to some authorities, the following barbed remark was made by George William Russell (1853–1919), the Liberal under-secretary:

'Mamma, are Tories born wicked, or do they grow wicked afterwards?'
'They are born wicked and grow worse.'

In the Proverbs section of the Bible, 10:1, these telling words are to be found:

A wise son maketh a glad father; but a foolish son is the heaviness of his mother.

Also in the Bible are the following lines that remain enduringly familiar. In the Old Testament, Exodus 20:1 commands:

Honour thy father and thy mother; that thy days may be long upon the land which the Lord thy God giveth thee.

And in the New Testament, St John's Gospel 19:26 says:

Woman, behold thy son! . . . Behold thy mother!

The mystical poet and artist William Blake (1757–1827) penned these lines in his moving poem entitled 'Infant Sorrow':

My mother groan'd, my father wept,
Into the dangerous world I leapt;
Helpless, naked, piping loud,
Like a fiend hid in a cloud.

Robert Browning (1812–1889) brought a touch of realism to poetry when it had become stereotyped in a hackneyed Romantic mould. This young girl's lament appears in 'A Blot on the 'Scutcheon', published in 1843:

I was so young, I loved him so, I had
No mother, God forgot me, and I fell.

Moving, too, but in a very different way, is the verse by Samuel Taylor Coleridge (1772–1834), taken from his *Sonnets*, with the rather ungainly title, 'To a Friend who asked how I felt when the nurse first presented my infant to me':

So for the mother's sake the child was dear,
And dearer was the mother for the child.

Many a child — and adult, too, — has delighted in reciting the next lines, mistakenly believing them to be an old nursery rhyme. In fact they were written in 1922 by the poet and novelist Walter de la Mare (1873-1956), in 'Come Hither':

My mother said that I never should,
Play with the gypsies in the wood;
If I did, she would say,
Naughty girl to disobey.

That master of nonsense verse, Hilaire Belloc (1870-1953), was responsible for this piece of light-hearted advice to mothers everywhere:

Mothers of large families (who claim to common sense)
Will find a Tiger will repay the trouble and expense.

While Lewis Carroll (1832–1898) was not so enamoured of young children that he could not also offer the following suggestion to mothers in his book *Alice in Wonderland*:

DADDY.

" Why do your big tears fall, Daddy,
Mother's not far away,
I often seem to hear her voice
Falling across my play,
And it sometimes makes me cry, Daddy,
To think that it's none of it true,
Till I fall asleep to dream, Daddy,
Of home and Mother and you ;
For I've got you, and you've got me,
So everything seems right,
We're all the world to each other, Daddy,
For Mother, dear Mother, once told me so."

WORDS BY PERMISSION OF BOOSEY & Co

Queen of the Earth.

An angel in all but name is she,
O'er life her vigil keeping,
Whose wings are spread o'er each cradle bed,
Where the hopes of earth lie sleeping.

Speak roughly to your little boy
And beat him when he sneezes,
He only does it to annoy
Because he knows it teases.

These lines were in fact a parody of the poem 'Speak Gently', a piece of improving verse by the Philadelphia poet David Bates. Benjamin Disraeli (1804–1881), the flamboyant politician and writer who was famous for his *bon mots* — in particular 'Variety is the mother of enjoyment', which can be found in his first novel,

Vivian Grey (1826) — also came out with this splendid remark when addressing a banquet at Glasgow University in November 1873:

> *An author who speaks about his own books is almost as bad as a mother who talks about her own children!*

One of the most famous Victorian ballads of young life cut short was 'Little Jim' by Edward Farmer, which gave rise to many irreverent parodies. Perhaps the best known is the following stanza:

> *I have no pain, dear mother now*
> *But, oh, I am so dry;*
> *O take me to a brewery*
> *And leave me there to die.*

There is also a nice touch of humour to be found in the verses entitled 'The Coquet Mother and the Coquet Daughter' by the poet John Gay (1685–1732) and although much of it is probably unfamiliar, these lines have a habit of being quoted:

> *Look ye, Mother, she cry'd,*
> *You instruct me in Pride,*
> *And Men by Good-manners are won.*
> *She who trifles with all*
> *Is less likely to fall*
> *Than she who but trifles with one!*

On a more serious note, the poet and hymn-writer Ann Gilbert (1782-1866) wrote these lovely lines in 1804 as one of her 'Original Poems for Infant Minds':

> *Who ran to help me when I fell,*
> *And would some pretty story tell,*
> *Or kiss the place to make it well?*
> *My mother.*

The Roman poet and satirist, Horace (65–8 BC), showed he

knew how to flatter women in his four excellent collections of Odes composed around 19 BC:

> O *matre pulchra filia pulchrior*
> (O fairer daughter of a fair mother.)

Anne Hunter (1742–1821) recalled her childhood in a famous song called 'My Mother Binds My Hair', one of several of her works which the composer Haydn set to music. Few people who recite the following words are probably aware of their origin in a song:

> *My mother bids me bind my hair,*
> *With bands of rosy hue,*
> *Tie up my sleeves with ribbons rare,*
> *And lace my bodice blue.*

That great storyteller Rudyard Kipling (1865–1936) possessed a remarkable insight into the human character. These famous words come from a poem entitled, 'Mary, Pity Women'. Over the years, variants of the lines have frequently been recorded.

Nice while it lasted, an' now it is over ——
Tear out your 'eart an' good-bye to your lover!
What's the use o' grievin', when the mother that bore you
(Mary, pity women!) knew it all before you?

Another distinguished English man of letters, John Masefield (1878–1967), whose poems and stories about the sea have assured him a secure place in literature, wrote these heart-felt lines in memory of his mother, 'C.L.M.':

In the dark womb where I began
My mother's life made me a man.
Through all the months of human birth
Her beauty fed my common earth.
I cannot see, nor breathe, nor stir,
But through the death of some of her.

A.A. Milne (1882–1956), creator of the immortal Pooh, was also a fine playwright and poet, and my own mother used to delight in reading me the following lines from 'Disobedience', a poem from the collection *When We Were Very Young* (1924) — as a gentle hint, I suspect:

James James
Morrison Morrison
Weatherby George Dupree
Took great
Care of his Mother
Though he was only three.

John Milton (1608–1674) was responsible for the phrase 'the mother of mankind', which is widely associated with Eve. It is to be found in his great work, *Paradise Lost* (1667), I:34.

The infernal serpent; he it was, whose guile,
Stirr'd up with envy and revenge, deceived
The mother of mankind.

There are some redoubtable mothers to be found in the works

of Sir Walter Scott (1771–1832), several of them not unlike his own mother, Anne Rutherford, a daughter of the Professor of Medicine at Edinburgh University. Two extracts must suffice. In 'Lullaby to an Infant Chief', he writes:

Oh hush thee, my baby, thy sire was a knight,
Thy mother a lady, both lovely and bright.

While in his novel *Rokeby* (1811) are to be found the well-known lines:

See yon pale stripling! when a boy,
A mother's pride, a father's joy!

Not surprisingly, perhaps, the most quoted of all authors where mothers are concerned is the great Bard himself, William Shakespeare (1564–1616). Here is a selection of his most famous words on the subject.

Thou has never in thy life
Show'd thy dear mother any courtesy;
When she — poor hen! fond of no second brood —
Has cluck'd thee to the wars, and safely home,
Loaden with honour.

Coriolanus v.iii.160

O wonderful son, that can so astonish a mother!
Hamlet, Prince of Denmark, iii.ii.347

My father compounded with my mother under the dragon's tail, and my nativity was under Ursa Major, so that it follows I am rough and lecherous. 'Sfoot! I should have been that I am, had the maidenliest star in the firmament twinkled on my bastardising.

King Lear, i.ii.132

DON PEDRO: *Out of question, you were born in a merry hour.*
BEATRICE: *No, sure, my lord, my mother cried; but then*

WOULD YOU DO IT?

there was a star danced, and under that was I born.
Much Ado About Nothing, II.i.348

PARIS: *Younger than she are happy mothers made.*
CAPULET: *And too soon marr'd are those so early made.*
Romeo and Juliet, I.ii.12

Thou art thy mother's glass, and she in thee,
Calls back the lovely April of her prime.
Sonnets, 3.9

Those last lines always remind me of a lovely phrase from the greatest of Latin poets, Virgil (70–19 BC), who wrote in his *Aeneid* (19 BC):

Incipe, parve puer, risu cognoscere matrem.
(Begin, baby boy, to recognise your mother with a smile.)

The acerbic George Bernard Shaw (1856–1950), whose father was improvident and his mother an energetic and musically-minded woman from whom he inherited his strength of character, made this now-famous observation through the figure of Tanner in the play, *Man and Superman* (1902):

> *The true artist will let his wife starve, his children go barefoot, his mother drudge for his living at seventy, sooner than work at anything but his art.*

Alfred Lord Tennyson (1809–1892), the master of Victorian sentimental verse, follows hard on the heels of Shakespeare, for he once remarked facetiously to his friend Carlyle, 'I don't think that since Shakespeare there has been such a master of the English language as I — to be sure I have nothing to say.' In fact, of course, he had a great deal to say, as the durability of his poetry has proved. These following lines are from *The Princess* (1847):

> *Happy he*
> *With such a mother! faith in womankind*
> *Beats with his blood, and trust in all things high*
> *Comes easy to him, and tho' he trip and fall*
> *He shall not blind his soul with clay.*

Oscar Wilde (1854–1900), whose mother, Lady Jane, was herself a distinguished writer, naturally enough had a thing or two to say about mothers. His most enduring remark is surely this exchange in the play *A Woman of No Importance* (1893):

LORD ILLINGWORTH: *People's mothers always bore me to death. All women become like their mothers. That is their tragedy.*
MRS ALLONBY: *No man does. That is his!*

And to end this brief catalogue of quotations, two most appropriate lines from the pen of William Wordsworth (1770–1850), who lost his mother when still young. In *The Prelude* (1805), he speaks not only of his own parent, but of the mother of *every* man and woman:

> *My honoured Mother, she who was the heart*
> *And hinge of all our learnings and our loves.*

A Ghostly Story

★★

The following story was told by the Scottish anthropologist and author, Lewis Spence (1874–1955).

I was born in the midst of a terrible storm, and this seemed to bind Mother and me together as creatures of one thought — a bond which lasted through our lives.

When I grew to manhood and life opened new vistas that took me away from her companionship, I know that her love followed me like a constant prayer. The years separated us, but never lessened the beautiful understanding between us.

I was in South America at the time of her passing. On that night I had retired early and slept soundly until about four o'clock, when I was suddenly awakened by my mother's presence in my room!

My bed faced the east, and was just opposite a closed door. That door quietly opened and Mother entered, coming slowly towards me with outstretched hands, speaking softly and, as was her custom, calling me by my first Christian name:

'Jamie, Jamie.'

I raised myself upon my pillow, supporting myself upon my elbows.

'Mother!' I exclaimed.

She came closer, and I could feel her soft hand as she leaned over my pillow. Hers was a palpitating, living presence. I did not close my eyes; they followed her form until she disappeared again through the door opposite, smiling and calling:

'Jamie, Jamie, goodbye!'

As soon as my strength returned, I rose, dressed and went downstairs. There, a little later, my wife found me, my face buried in my hands.

'What is it?' she asked quietly, and I told her.

97

She attempted to cheer me, saying it must be merely a dream. But I knew better.

A few hours later a telegram arrived to confirm what Mother had come to tell me.

She was gone — she had come to say goodbye.

Ghost Stories
October, 1938

MOTHER MACHREE (3).

Ev'ry sorrow or care in the dear days gone by,
Was made bright by the light of the smile in your eye;
Like a candle that's set in a window at night,
Your fond love has cheered me and guided me right.

'Dearest Mother'

✦✦✦

The letter printed below has been described as the most moving ever written by a son to his mother. It was never actually posted, but was found among the belongings of a Second World War RAF bomber pilot, after his plane had been reported missing in the Spring of 1940. As the letter was left open — a wartime security instruction — it was read by the young man's station commander, who was so moved by the sentiments expressed that he asked the mother for permission to publish it as an inspiration to others. This permission was granted, and the letter appeared in *The Times* of 18 June, 1940. Such was its impact that requests for copies poured into the newspaper and within a month about 500,000 copies had been sold. The letter became one of the legends of the war.

Subsequently, the identity of the young writer was revealed as Pilot Officer Vivian Alan Rosewarne, the only son of Mrs Lillian Rosewarne. He was killed with his crew of 36(B) Squadron during the evacuation of Dunkirk. A member of the same Squadron commented, after the authorship of the letter had been made known, that, on the surface, P.O. Rosewarne was the most unlikely member of the Squadron to have written it. 'He possessed tremendous vitality and a seemingly insatiable urge to enjoy every moment of life to the full,' said Group Captain Ronald Coulson, 'almost as if he did have a premonition, although he denies this in his letter . . . I am certain that when he and his crew met their deaths a few months later they went to the limits and probably beyond in order to ensure the success of their mission.'

Dearest Mother,

Though I feel no premonition at all, events are moving rapidly,

An enormously popular First World War card by the famous cartoonist, Lawson Wood.

and I have instructed that this letter be forwarded to you should I fail to return from one of the raids which we shall shortly be called upon to undertake.

You must hope on for a month, but at the end of that time you must accept the fact that I have handed my task over to the extremely capable hands of my comrades of the Royal Air Force, as so many splendid fellows have already done.

First, it will comfort you to know that my role in this war has been of the greatest importance. Our patrols far out over the North Sea have helped to keep the trade routes clear for our convoys and supply ships, and on one occasion our information was instrumental in saving the lives of the men in a crippled lighthouse relief ship.

Though it will be difficult for you, you will disappoint me if you do not at least try to accept the facts dispassionately, for I shall have done my duty to the utmost of my ability. No man can do more, and no one calling himself a man could do less.

I have always admired your amazing courage in the face of continual setbacks; in the way you have given me as good an education and background as anyone in the country; and always kept up appearances without ever losing faith in the future.

My death would not mean that your struggle has been in vain. Far from it. It means that your sacrifice is as great as mine.

Those who serve England must expect nothing from her; we debase ourselves if we regard our country as merely a place in which to eat and sleep.

History resounds with illustrious names who have given all, yet their sacrifice has resulted in the British Empire, where there is a measure of peace, justice, and freedom for all, and where a higher standard of civilisation has evolved, and is still evolving, than anywhere else.

But this is not only concerning our own land. Today we are faced with the greatest organised challenge to Christianity and civilisation that the world has ever seen, and I count myself lucky and honoured to be the right age and fully trained to throw my weight into the scale.

For this I have to thank you. Yet there is more work for you to do. The Home Front will still have to stand united for years after the war is won.

For all that can be said against it, I still maintain that this war is a very good thing; every individual is having the chance to give and dare all for his principle like the martyrs of old.

However long the time may be, one thing can never be altered — I shall have lived and died an Englishman. Nothing else matters one jot, nor can anything ever change it.

You must not grieve for me, for if you really believe in religion and all that it entails, that would be hypocrisy. I have no fear of death; only a queer elation . . . I would have it no other way.

The universe is so vast and so ageless that the life of one man can only be justified by the measure of his sacrifice. We are sent to this world to acquire a personality and a character to take with us that can never be taken from us. Those who just eat and sleep, prosper and procreate, are no better than animals if all their lives they are at peace.

I firmly and absolutely believe that evil things are sent into the world to try us; they are sent deliberately by our Creator to test our metal because He knows what is good for us. The Bible is full of cases where the easy way out has been discarded for moral principles.

I count myself fortunate in that I have seen the whole country and known men of every calling. But with the final test of war, I consider my character fully developed.

Thus at my early age, my earthly mission is already fulfilled and I am prepared to die with just one regret, and only one — that I could not devote myself to making your declining years more happy by being with you. But you will live in peace and freedom and I shall have directly contributed to that, so here again my life will not have been in vain.

Your loving Son.

For the Love of Mother

A pot-pourri of literary extracts

★★★

A LETTER TO MY MOTHER

Miss Clarissa Harlowe to her Mother

Honoured Madam,

No self-convinced criminal ever approached her angry and just judge with greater awe, nor with a truer contrition, than I do you by these lines.

Indeed, I must say, that if the matter of my humble prayer had not respected my future welfare, I had not dared to take this liberty. But my heart is set upon it, as upon anything next to God's Almighty forgiveness necessary for me. Had my happy sister known my distress, she would not have wrung my heart, as she has done, by a severity which I must needs think unkind and unsisterly.

But complaint of any unkindness from her belongs not to me: yet as she is pleased to write that it must be seen that my penitence is less owing to disappointment than to true conviction, permit me, Madam, to insist upon it, that if such a plea can be allowed me, I am actually *entitled* to the blessing I sue for; since my humble prayer is founded upon a true and unfeigned repentance: and this you will the readier believe, if the creature who never, to the best of her remembrance, told her mamma a wilful falsehood may be credited, when she declares, as she does in the most solemn manner, that she met the seducer with a determination not to go off with him: that the rash step was owing more to compulsion than infatuation, and that her heart was so little in it, that she repented and grieved from the moment she found herself in his power; and for every moment after, for several weeks *before* she had any cause from him to apprehend the usage she met with.

Wherefore, on my knees, my ever-honoured Mamma (for on

103

CLARISSA.

The old dragon straddled up to her.

Clarissa Harlowe, the heroine of Samuel Richardson's novel.

my knees I write this letter), I do most humbly beg your blessing: say but, in so many words (I ask you not, Madam, to call me your daughter), *Lost, unhappy wretch, I forgive you! and may God bless you!* That is all! Let me, on a blessed scrap of paper, but see one sentence to this effect, under your dear hand, that I may hold it to my heart in my most trying struggles, and I shall think it a passport to Heaven. And if I do not too much presume, and it were WE instead of I, and both your honoured names to it, I should then have nothing more to wish. Then would I say, 'Great and merciful God! Thou seest here in this paper Thy poor, unworthy creature absolved by her justly-offended parents. Oh! join, for my Redeemer's sake, Thy all-gracious *fiat*, and receive a repentant sinner to the arms of Thy mercy.'

I can conjure you, Madam, by no subject of motherly tenderness, that will not in the opinion of my severe censurers (before whom this humble address must appear), add to reproach: Let me therefore, for God's sake, prevail upon you to pronounce me blest and forgiven, since you will thereby sprinkle comfort through the last hours of your

Clarissa Harlowe

Samuel Richardson (1689–1761)
Novelist and 'champion of women'.
The History of Clarissa Harlowe (1748)

*   *   *

A LETTER TO MY DAUGHTER

Mrs Henrietta Maria Honora Andrews to Miss Shamela Andrews

Dear Child,

Why will you give such way to your Passion? How could you imagine I should be such a Simpleton, as to upbraid thee with being thy Mother's own Daughter! When I advised you not to be guilty of Folly, I meant no more than that you should take care to be well-paid before-hand, and not trust to Promises, which a Man seldom keeps, after he hath had his wicked Will. And seeing you have a rich Fool to deal with, your not making a good Market will be the more inexcusable; indeed, with such Gentlemen as Parson Williams, there is more to be said; for they have nothing to give, and are commonly otherwise the best Sort of Men. I am glad to hear you read good Books, pray continue so to do. I have enclosed you one of Mr Whitefield's Sermons, and also the Dealings with him, and am,

> Your affectionate Mother,
> Henrietta Maria &c.

> Henry Fielding (1707–1754)
> Novelist and burlesque writer.
> *Shamela* (1741), a parody of *Pamela* by Samuel Richardson

✳   ✳   ✳

A DISCUSSION CONCERNING BREECHES

We should begin, said my father, turning himself half round in bed, and shifting his pillows a little towards my mother's, as he opened the debate — We should begin to think, Mrs Shandy, of putting this boy into breeches.

We should so — said my mother. — We defer it, my dear, quoth my father, shamefully.

I think we do, Mr Shandy — said my mother.

— Not but the child looks extremely well, said my father, in his vests and tunics.

— He does look very well in them, replied my mother.

— And for that reason it would be almost a Sin, added my father, to take him out of 'em.

— It would so, said my mother — But indeed he is growing a very tall lad, rejoined my father.

— He is very tall for his age, indeed, said my mother.

— I can not (making two syllables of it) imagine, quoth my father, who the deuce he takes after.

I cannot conceive, for my life — said my mother.

Humph! — said my father.

(The dialogue ceased for a moment.)

— I am very short myself — continued my father gravely.

You are very short, Mr Shandy, said my mother.

Humph! quoth my father to himself, a second time: in mutter-ing which, he plucked his pillow a little further from my mother's — and turning about again, there was an end of the debate for three minutes and a half.

— When he gets these breeches made, cried my father in a higher tone, he'll look like a beast in 'em.

— He will be very awkward in them at first, replied my mother.

— And 'twill be lucky, if that's the worst on't, added my father.

It will be very lucky, answered my mother.

I suppose, replied my father — making some pause first — he'll be exactly like other people's children?

Exactly, said my mother.

I shall be sorry for that, added my father: and so the debate stopped.

Laurence Sterne (1713–1768)
Humorist and novelist.
The Life and Opinions of Tristram Shandy (1759)

*   *   *

A MOTHER'S DESIGN

'Is our new neighbour married or single?' enquired Mr Bennet.

'Oh, single, my dear, to be sure! A single man of large fortune; four or five thousand a year. What a fine thing for our girls!'

'How so? how can it affect them?'

'My dear Mr Bennet,' replied his wife, 'how can you be so tiresome? You must know that I am thinking of his marrying one of them.'

'Is that his design in settling here?'

'Design? nonsense, how can you talk so! But it is very likely that he *may* fall in love with one of them, and therefore you must visit him as soon as he comes.'

'I see no occasion for that. You and the girls may go — or you may send them by themselves, which perhaps will be still better; for as you are as handsome as any of them, Mr Bingley might like you the best of the party.'

'My dear, you flatter me. I certainly *have* had my share of beauty, but I do not pretend to be anything extraordinary now. When a woman has five grown-up daughters, she ought to give over thinking of her own beauty.'

'In such cases, a woman has not often much beauty to think of,' Mr Bennet replied.

Jane Austen (1775–1817)
Novelist and observer of human nature.
Pride and Prejudice (1813)

What Mother Had Always Wanted.

A story of a longing that lasted through the years.

By LINDA BUNTYN WILLIE.

Illustrations

by

J. E. Sutcliffe.

" A diamond ! " Mother half whispered. " I was hoping he'd give you a ring, but I never thought of a diamond."

I JUST hate to show it to Mother ! " Laura held up her left hand and watched the light play on the diamond on the engagement-finger.

Laura turned on her sharply. " Why didn't you finish what you started to say ? Why didn't you say that she was fat and plain and had rough, red hands from working for us, that would look funny with rings on them ? "

Viva shrugged her shoulders as she

'What Mother had Always Wanted' a story about Mothering Sunday from Pearson's Magazine, *March 1931.*

*   *   *

OUR MOTHERS

Round the idea of one's mother, the mind of man clings with fond affection. It is the first thought stamped upon our infant hearts, when yet soft and capable to receiving the most profound impressions, and all the after feelings of the world are more or less light in comparison. I do not know that even in our old age we do not look back to that feeling as the sweetest we have ever known through life.

Our passions and our wilfulness may lead us far from the object of our filial love; we may learn even to pain her heart, to oppose her wishes, to violate her commands; we may become wild, headstrong and angry at her councils or opposition; but when death has stilled her monitory voice, and nothing but calm memory remains to recapitulate her good deeds, affection, like a flower beaten to the ground by a past storm, raises up her head and smiles amid her tears.

Round that idea, as we have said, the mind clings with fond affection and even when the earliest period of our loss forces memory to be silent, fancy takes the place of remembrance, and twines the image of our dead parent with a garland of graces, and beauties, and virtues, which we doubt not that she possessed.

Charles Dickens (1812–1870)
All Year Round, March 1860

*   *   *

THE MATERNAL INSTINCT

How his mother nursed him, and dressed him, and lived upon him; how she drove away all nurses, and would scarce allow any hand but her own to touch him; how she considered that the

Elizabeth Ann came rushing into the house with
a wild howl. "He—he—hitted me!"

greatest favour she could confer upon his godfather, Major Dobbin, was to allow the Major occasionally to dandle him, need not be told here.

This child was her being. Her existence was a maternal caress. She enveloped the feeble and unconscious creature with love and worship. It was her life which the baby drank in from her bosom.

Of nights, and when alone, she had stealthy and intense raptures of motherly love, such as God's marvellous care has awarded to the female instinct — joys how far higher and lower than reason — blind, beautiful devotions which only women's hearts know.

It was William Dobbin's task to muse upon these movements of Amelia's, and to watch her heart; and if his love made him divine almost all the feelings which agitated it, alas! he could see with a fatal perspicuity that there was no place there for him. And so, gently, he bore his fate, knowing it, and content to bear it.

William Makepeace Thackeray (1811–1863)
Journalist and author.
Vanity Fair (1847)

*　　*　　*

A MOTHER OF QUALITY

Ralph Touchett was a philosopher, but nevertheless he knocked at his mother's door (at a quarter to seven) with a good deal of eagerness. Even philosophers have their preferences, and it must be admitted that of his progenitors his father ministered most to his sense of the sweetness of filial dependence. His father, as he had often said to himself, was the more motherly; his mother, on the other hand, was paternal, and even, according to the slang of the day, gubernatorial. She was nevertheless very fond of her only child and had always insisted on his spending three months of the

Left: A delightful study by Mabel Lucie Attwell of mother and child, April 1926.

113

year with her. Ralph rendered perfect justice to her affection and knew that in her thoughts and her thoroughly arranged and servanted life, his turn always came after the other nearest subjects of her solicitude, the various punctualities of performance of the workers of her will.

He found her completely dressed for dinner, but she embraced her boy with her gloved hands and made him sit on the sofa beside her. She enquired scrupulously about her husband's health and about the young man's own, and, receiving no very brilliant account of either, remarked that she was more than ever convinced of the wisdom in not exposing oneself to the English climate. In this case she might also have given way. Ralph smiled at the idea of his mother's giving way, but made no point of reminding her that her own infirmity, such as it was, was not the result of the English climate, from which she absented herself for a considerable part of each year.

Henry James (1843–1916)
Novelist of social life.
Portrait of a Lady (1880)

*   *   *

ONE OF LIFE'S TRAGEDIES

Lizer was some months short of twenty-one when her third child was born. The pickle factory had discarded her some time before, and since that her trade had consisted in odd jobs of charing.

Lizer's self was also scarcely what it had been. The red of her cheeks, once bounded only by the eyes and the mouth, had shrunk to a spot in the depth of each hollow; gaps had been driven in her big, white teeth; even the snub nose had run to a point, and the fringe of hair hung dry and ragged, while the body outline was as a sack's.

Right: Making gardening a little easier for mums and dads—a typical W. Heath Robinson piece of ingenuity, from The Merrythought, *February 1929.*

MY HINTS TO AMATEUR GARDENERS.

NEW METHODS OF LIGHTENING A HEAVY SOIL.

THE DREADFUL BALLAD OF A TALKIE-RUINED HOME

A MOTHER stood in tears amid the ruins of her home
Beseeching of her menfolk dear that evening not to
    roam ;
Her first-born rose and struck her, but as he reached
    the door
The woman on her bended knees her husband did
    implore—

    " Don't take my boy to the Talkies !
      It's puttin' ideas in 'is 'ead,
    'E makes the most 'orrible faces,
      And sleeps with a gun in 'is bed.
    'E uses outlandish American words,
    It's nothin' but " bootleggers," " babies," and " birds,"
      'E says I've an English accent
      An' it's not that I mind the snub,
    But I want my boy to be British,
      So take 'im with you to the pub ! "

At home, the children lay in her arms or tumbled at her heels, puling and foul. Whenever she was near it, there was the mangle to be turned; for lately Billy's mother had exhibited a strange weakness, sometimes collapsing with a gasp in the act of brisk or prolonged exertion, and often leaning on whatever stood hard by and grasping at her side. This ailment she treated, when she had twopence, in such terms as made her smell of gin and peppermint; and more than once this circumstance had inflamed the breast of Billy, her son, who was morally angered by this boozing away of money that should have been his for the same purpose . . .

> Arthur Morrison (1863–1945)
> Novelist and social reformer.
> *Tales of Mean Streets* (1894)

✻   ✻   ✻

A SECOND MARRIAGE

It was on an evening when they were alone in their plain suburban residence, where life was not blue but brown, that she ultimately broke silence, qualifying her announcement of a probable second marriage by assuring her son that it would not take place for a long time to come, when he would be living quite independently of her.

The boy thought the idea a very reasonable one, and asked if she had chosen anybody. She hesitated; and he seemed to have a misgiving. He hoped his stepfather would be a gentleman, he said.

'Not what you call a gentleman,' she answered timidly. 'He'll be much as I was before I knew your father'; and by degrees she acquainted him with the details of the simple countryman. The youth's face remained fixed for a moment; then he flushed, leant on the table, and burst into passionate tears.

Left: A mother's plea—one of A.P. Herbert's amusing ballads from Punch, *March 1931.*

His mother went up to him, kissed all of his face that she could get at, and patted his back as if he were still the baby he once had been, crying herself the while. When he had somewhat recovered from his paroxysm he went hastily to his own room and fastened the door.

Parleyings were attempted through the keyhole, outside which she waited and listened. It was long before he would reply, and when he did it was to say sternly at her from within:

'I am ashamed of you! It will ruin me! A miserable boor! A churl! A clown! It will degrade me in the eyes of all the gentlemen of England.'

'Say no more — perhaps I am wrong! I will struggle against it!' she cried miserably.

Thomas Hardy (1840–1928)
Novelist of country life.
Life's Little Ironies (1894)

*   *   *

A SHAMEFUL SECRET

Her mind was full of an adventure through which she had passed seven years previously, when she was thirteen and a little girl at school. For several days, then, she had been ruthlessly mortifying her mother by complaints about the meals. Her fastidious appetite could not be suited. At last, one noon when the child had refused the whole of a plenteous dinner, Mrs Lessways had burst into tears and, slapping four pennies down on the table, had cried, 'Here! I fairly give you up! Go out and buy your own dinner! Then perhaps you'll get what you want!' And the child, without an instant's hesitation, had seized the coins and gone out, hatless, and bought food at a little tripe-shop that was also an eating-house, and consumed it there; and then in grim silence returned home. Both mother and daughter had been stupefied and frightened by the boldness of the daughter's initiative, by her amazing, flaunting disregard of filial decency. Mrs Lessways would not have related the episode to anybody upon any consideration whatever. It was a shameful secret, never even referred to. But Mrs Lessways had unmistakably though indirectly referred to it when in anger she had said to her daughter, aged twenty: 'I suppose her ladyship will be consulting her own lawyer next!' Hilda had understood, and she had blushed.

Arnold Bennett (1867–1931)
Novelist and critic.
Hilda Lessways (1911)

*   *   *

UNLOVED

In her arms lay the delicate baby. Its deep blue eyes, always looking at her unblinking, seemed to draw her innermost thoughts out of her. She no longer loved her husband; she had not wanted this child to come, and there it lay in her arms and pulled at her heart. She felt as if the navel string that had connected its frail little body with hers had not been broken.

A wave of hot love went over her to the infant. She held it close to her face and breast. With all her force, with all her soul, she would make up to it for having brought it into the world unloved. She would love it all the more now it was here; carry it in her love. Its clear, knowing eyes gave her pain and fear. Did it know all about her? When it lay under her heart, had it been listening then? Was there a reproach in the look? She felt the marrow melt in her bones, with fear and pain.

D.H. Lawrence (1885–1930)
Novelist and poet.
Sons and Lovers (1913)

*   *   *

ONE THING AFTER ANOTHER . . .

But the struggle she'd had to bring up those six little children and keep herself to herself. Terrible it had been! Then, just when they were old enough to go to school, her husband's sister came to stop with them to help things along, and she hadn't been there more than two months when she fell down a flight of steps and hurt her spine. And for five years Ma Parker had another baby — such a one for crying! — to look after. Then young Maudie went wrong and took her sister Alice with her; the two boys emigrated, and young Jim went to India with the army, and Ethel, the youngest, married a good-for-nothing little waiter who died of ulcers the year little Lennie was born. And now little Lennie — my grandson . . .

The piles of dirty cups, dirty dishes, were washed and dried. The ink-black knives were cleaned with a piece of potato and finished off with a piece of cork. The table was scrubbed, and the dresser and the sink that had sardine tails swimming in it . . .

He'd never been a strong child — never from the first. He'd been one of those fair babies that everybody took for a girl. Silvery fair curls he had, blue eyes, and a little freckle like a diamond on one side of his nose. The trouble she and Ethel had had to rear that child! The things out of the newspapers they tried him with! Every Sunday morning Ethel would read aloud while Ma Parker did her washing.

'Dear Sir — Just a line to let you know my little Myrtil was laid out for dead . . . After four bottles . . . gained 8 lbs in 9 weeks, *and is still putting it on.*'

Katherine Mansfield (1888–1923)
Short-story writer.
Life of Ma Parker (1922)

*　　　*　　　*

Right: There's nothing new under the sun! A cartoonist's ideas of some future hairstyles for mothers and daughters, made in 1926, predicts the Punk era with uncanny accuracy.

The latest shingle is
called the "Cock's Comb."

Why not later the
"Cockatoo,"

the "Horse's Mane,"

the "Cow's Horn,"

the "Yew Tree,"

the "Grass Field,"

the "Sitting Hen,"

the "Flying Pigeon,"   or the "Morning Sun" ?

WHY NOT ?

THE BREEDING OF LUSTFUL ANIMALS

'The English are so serious,' she would say, putting her arms round Septimus, her cheek against his.

Love between man and woman was repulsive to Shakespeare. The business of copulation was filthy to him before the end. But she must have children. They had been married five years.

She must have a son like Septimus, she said. But nobody could be like Septimus; so gentle; so serious; so clever. Could she not read Shakespeare too? Was Shakespeare a difficult author? she asked.

One cannot bring children into a world like this. One cannot perpetuate suffering, or increase the breed of these lustful animals, who have no lasting emotions, but only whims and vanities, eddying them now this way, now that.

> Virginia Woolf (1882–1941)
> Novelist and essayist.
> *Mrs Dalloway* (1925)

*   *   *

A LADY OF TASTE

I associate my mother with remoteness, which I did not at all resent, and with a smell of eau-de-cologne. If I could have tasted her, I am sure she would have tasted of wheaten biscuits.

My mother would pay occasional state visits to the nursery. But her remoteness, her wonderful lack of possessive instinct, was made much easier for her to achieve by the presence of Nanny. I never remember being afraid of her.

> Graham Greene (1904–   )
> Novelist and critic.
> *A Sort of Life* (1971)

*   *   *

BRITISH MOTHER'S BIG FLIGHT

'Of course it is wonderful to be the first mother to fly the North Pole with her baby! But I never thought people would make such a fuss of me! I'm sure any other mother would have done the same. And I hope before long every British mother will be able to fly to the North Pole with her baby. The engine was wonderful!

'I hope none of you think I did it for the publicity. I just couldn't believe my eyes when I saw my name in the papers — and everything. I dunno — I just had to do it. I felt I had to strike a blow for British motherhood — and the British carburettor — and everything. The engine was wonderful. Lord Merridew's been ever so kind. Baby was fine. Of course I used Merriol lubricating oil . . .

'Now perhaps you'd like to hear what it felt like to be over the North Pole — just a British mother with her baby. Of course we couldn't *see* the North Pole. We were flying blind — clouds and everything. But somehow I just knew we were there. And — I dunno — I got a sort of lump in my throat thinking of mother, and England, and everything, and so I held baby over the side, and I said, "There, Tiddles, you'll be able to tell your children you were the first baby to be sick over the Arctic Circle!"'

A.P. Herbert (1890–1971)
Humorist and politician.
Mild and Bitter (1945)

*   *   *

WE TWO TOGETHER

'I have something to say to you, my son. Come closer to me and hear it. It is not a sad thing in itself or to me, but sad, I fear, to you. It is the sadness we knew was coming nearer. Yes, my days are numbered, Rosebery; not as they must be for the old, but actually for me. My heart has done its work, and can do no more.

And I daresay it has done enough. The doctors were plain with me, when they saw I would brook nothing else. They wanted to see you or your father, but I could say my own word. And now I have said it, no more must be asked of me. My life is spent, and I must lean on others at the last.'

Miranda's voice broke on a querulous note, but with no undertone of despair. She had had her time, and would see nothing tragic in its close.

The two men came to her side.

'Miranda, my wife, so it has come, what we have seen ahead. I hoped I should overtake it, but it has held its own. For both of us it is the end.'

'Not for you. You have further to go, though perhaps not so far. You will have the children. For you it is not the worst. It is for my son that it is that.'

'Mother, it is. But I would not have it otherwise. It is the mark of what I have had. Together we have gone our way; together we will go on, even though with a veil between; even though the one be taken and the other left.'

Ivy Compton-Burnett (1884–1969)
Novelist of family life.
Mother and Son (1955)

*   *   *

LIKE YOUNG LOVERS

A moment later Ma turned to reach from a cupboard a new tin of salt and Pop, watching her upstretched figure as it revealed portions of enormous calves, suddenly felt a startling twinge of excitement in his veins. He immediately grasped Ma by her bosom and started squeezing her. Ma pretended to protest, giggling at the same time, but Pop continued to fondle her with immense, experienced enthusiasm, until finally she turned, yielded the great continent of her body to him and let him kiss her full on her soft, big mouth.

124

Pop prolonged this delicious experience as long as he had breath. He always felt more passionate in the kitchen. He supposed it was the smell of food. Ma sometimes told him it was a wonder he ever got any meals at all and that he ought to know, at his age, which he wanted most, meals or her.

'Both,' he always said. 'Often.'

H.E. Bates (1905–1974)
Country author and short-story writer.
The Darling Buds of May (1958)

*   *   *

AN INDESTRUCTIBLE GAIETY

Deserted, debt-ridden, flurried, bewildered, doomed by ambitions that never came off, yet our mother possessed an indestructible gaiety which welled up like a thermal spring. Her laughing, like her weeping, was instantaneous and childlike, and switched without warning — or memory. Her emotions were entirely without reserve; she clouted you one moment and hugged you the next — to the ruin of one's ragged nerves. If she knocked over a pot, or cut her finger, she let out a blood-chilling scream — then forgot about it immediately in a hop and skip or a song. I can still seem to hear her blundering about the kitchen: shrieks and howls of alarm, an occasional oath, a gasp of wonder, a sharp command to things to stay still. A falling coal would set her hair on end, a loud knock make her leap and yell, her world was a maze of small traps and snares acknowledged always by cries of dismay. One couldn't help jumping in sympathy with her, though one learned to ignore these alarms. They were, after all, no more than formal salutes to the devils that dogged her heels.

Laurie Lee (1914–   )
Poet and writer.
Cider with Rosie (1959)

125

THERE'S A LIGHT THAT'S BURNING IN
THE WINDOW (2).

There's a light that's burning in the window, of a little house
    upon the hill,
And the light will burn, and a heart will yearn, and it always
    will till I return,
For there's only one mother, I know she's waiting still,
And she'll always keep the light a-burning in the window of
    the house upon the hill.

MEMORIES ARE MADE OF THIS

When they came to Richard's room, his mother stood on the threshold and, with her fingers to her lips for no apparent reason, swung the door open. Compared with the rest of the house this was a bleak, untidy, almost schoolboy's room.

Richard's green pyjama trousers lay on the floor where he had stepped out of them. This was a sight familiar to Trudy from her several week-end excursions with Richard, of late months, to hotels up the Thames valley.

'So untidy,' said Richard's mother, shaking her head woefully. 'So untidy. One day, Trudy dear, we must have a real chat.'

> Muriel Spark (1918–   )
> Novelist and short-story writer.
> *A Member of the Family* (1967)

✲   ✲   ✲

PLEASANT DREAMS

It is time for bed. I have never suffered from night fears. I was never, that I can recall, afraid of the dark as a child.

My mother early impressed upon me that fear of the dark was a superstition from which God-fearing people did not suffer. I hardly needed God to protect me. My mother was an absolute defence against every terror.

> Iris Murdoch (1919–   )
> Novelist and philosopher.
> *The Sea, The Sea* (1978)

Acknowledgements

★★

I am grateful to a large number of people who helped make this book possible through their contribution of memories about their mothers and also by supplying the many delightful postcards and illustrations which decorate its pages. In particular, though, I must mention Bill Lofts for his research into the history of Mothering Sunday, C.D. Paramour for his help with the old verses and song sheets, and the staff at the British Museum and London Library who helped trace many of the texts and extracts quoted herein. My thanks, too, to Valentines of Dundee and Royle Publications Ltd for their help with information about Mother's Day cards, and Bamforth & Co for their delightful postcards. Also *The Times*, the *Daily Mail*, the *New York Times* and *Notes & Queries* for permission to quote from their pages, as well as the following British publishers for quotations: Macmillan & Co, Methuen, Hogarth Press, Chatto & Windus, Constable and Longmans.